PAWS FOR CONCERN

A Canine Confections Mystery

Amy Hueston

Copyright © 2020 by Amy Hueston

All rights reserved. No part of this book may be reproduced in any form or by any electronic or mechanical means including information storage and retrieval systems, without permission in writing from the author. The only exception is by a reviewer, who may quote short excerpts in a review.

Paw icons courtesy of Freepik on Flaticon.com.

ISBN: 978-1-944066-37-6

Printed in the United States

*To my dogs, my mother and my husband, I am forever appreciative.
This book is for all of you.*

Acknowledgments

I would like to thank my family, friends and the writing community for helping me bring this book into the world. In particular, I would like to thank my literary agent Julie Gwinn, Three Dog Bakery, editor Mel Hughes and South Florida Deputy Sheriff Tom Cuty. I couldn't have done this without you. Finally, I would also like to thank every single dog I have ever owned. Or, if I'm being completely honest … who has ever owned me.

CHAPTER ONE

I snatched the tray of Doggone Good Cupcakes off the display counter away from my aunt. "If you keep sampling the baked goods, the only thing I'll have to offer the dogs tomorrow will be espresso."

Aunt Mary's blue eyes twinkled and her smile widened. "I'm testing them to make sure they taste alright, Samantha. You said they're human grade..."

"But they're for the dogs. I'm opening a *dog* bakery, remember?"

Eight of the twelve mini-cupcakes were salvageable. The rest would have to be thrown out or given to my aunt. How she managed to eat like that without gaining an ounce was beyond me... I only needed to *look* at a cupcake and had to add an extra ten minutes to my morning jog.

I wrapped my hands around the pastry bag and squeezed gently over a cupcake, but nothing came out of the tip. Instead, the pile of pink creamy goodness inched up toward the large opening at the top of the bag and threatened to gush all over my hands.

Aunt Mary gestured with one manicured but slightly weathered hand. "If you overfill the pastry bag, the frosting will glop out."

"You'd think I'd have gotten the knack by now ..." Suddenly, a moment of the last-minute jitters set in. I looked at my aunt in wide-eyed panic and rambled. "Do you think I've made a mistake? What do *I* know about baking for dogs?"

"Samantha Armstrong! What is this nonsense coming from you? You researched it, you did taste-tests, you're good with business ... you'll be fine."

My heartbeat slowed a little. "Okay. *I'll be fine.*"

She busied herself with the "Enjoy espresso while your pooch enjoys a snack" sign on the counter. "And your baking skills will only improve with time."

"Yeah ... what?"

"I'm only teasing." She stepped back to inspect the placement of the sign, but her leg buckled under her. She winced in pain.

"Your knee!" I cried. I dropped the pastry bag on the counter and raced over. "Are you alright?" I reconsidered my brilliant idea of bringing her here to Canine Confections rather than making her stay home and ice her knee like the surgeon advised. Immediately, I guided her to the bench seating with down-filled cushions special ordered in Colefax and Fowler fabric. The cotton and silk tropical print depicting palm fronds and aqua and turquoise blooms cost a pretty penny, but this was Palm Beach after all. I just hoped Aunt Mary's investment would pay off.

I returned to the cupcakes while she looked around the cafe.

"It's elegantly cozy." She laid a finger to her chin. "Or is it *cozily elegant?*"

The sweet scent from the mixture of honey and cream cheese wafted through the air, hitting my nose with a distinct fragrance. It was a soothing smell that enveloped me in its warm embrace. If alone at home in my kitchen, I would have been content to stand at my counter for another couple hours at least. I went back to piping frosting and now that I had a handle on it, my usual confidence was back with a vengeance.

"Ah, beautiful!" I said to the swirl atop a cupcake.

I kept my eye on my aunt as I moved on to the next one and glanced at a shopper on the sidewalk of Worth Avenue ... a man with one of those oh-I-forgot-to-shave-yesterday faces peeked in Confections' large display window. He smiled and went on his way past the second of two palm trees that flank my storefront. I over-twisted the pastry bag, glopping frosting onto the sparkling floor—I love a man with day-old facial hair.

Aunt Mary, busy with the $125 napkin holder on the table, asked, "What are you going to do about replacing Trisha?"

Trisha, the young woman I'd hired who had the audacity to prefer moving to Nashville with her sexy musician boyfriend instead of staying in South Florida and working for me.

"I'm going to sift through the online job site soon as I have a minute." I organized the cupcakes onto a platter, tried to envision what the Barefoot Contessa would do, and couldn't. My baking skills were pretty good, but my eye for placement and decorating? Not so much.

Next, I unloaded a box of napkins and wiped sweat off my forehead. I wouldn't have minded another look-see at Mr. Sexy Stubble but all I spied were women in Lilly Pulitzer dresses and men wearing shoes so shiny the infamous Florida sunshine glistened off them. I glanced over at Aunt Mary as I pulled out another napkin. Her eyelids shut. We had left Whitehall Manor on Ocean Boulevard that morning at the crack of too-early-for-most-people.

I was so wired from my new life that I hardly noticed I'd been running on empty for a month. Next on my list would be finally adopting a dog. Peter was *allergic*. When I think that I procrastinated getting a dog because of the bad egg that used to be my boyfriend …

Aunt Mary opened her eyes, tried to stand up and groaned.

Horrified, I asked, "Why are you trying to get up on your own?"

"It's just tingling, that's all."

"I know you and when you say tingling, that means it hurts." I hurried over with an ice pack from the mini-freezer. "Hold this on your knee while I put the whipped cream back in the refrigerator and grab my keys."

"I don't want you running me home and having to drive all the way back here."

"It's ten minutes. I'll live."

"I'll call Alice to come get me."

I knew nothing of the kind of life where you can afford to have a personal assistant in case you need something.

"Though, I've been thinking about that lately," she said thoughtfully. "Do I really need to have someone on standby? It seems a waste of money."

This? From my aunt? The last time she talked like this, Uncle Joseph had been going through a short gambling spell and almost bankrupted them.

"Giving me the money to open Canine Confections isn't putting you in any kind of financial danger, right?" When she didn't answer, I repeated, "Right?" *Because if that's the case, I have a whole lot more to worry about if it fails.*

Aunt Mary scoffed. "Oh, stop."

"That's not an answer."

She reached into her purse and pressed a number which I could only assume was Alice on speed dial.

After she hung up, I said, "Will she stay with you until I come home later?"

"I don't need a babysitter." She latched onto my cheek with her thumb and forefinger and gave it a light squeeze.

"That house of yours is so big, it's like walking a marathon just making it to the kitchen from your bedroom."

"I'll stay on the patio. I'll be fine."

I didn't believe her. Or more to the point, I worried anyway.

"You know what?" I said. "I only have some paperwork to finish up. I'll just grab it off my desk and be ready to skedaddle out of here with you in a few minutes. Call Alice back and tell her you don't need her."

I packaged up the cupcakes and ran to the back office. When I returned to the café from the back room two minutes later, a young woman about my age was bouncing up and down on her toes in upscale sneakers. I pegged her in her early twenties, a few shades younger than my twenty-seven.

"Can I help you?" I asked. *And how did you get into my closed dog bakery?* I looked at the slight sheath of sweat on Aunt Mary's face and knew the answer.

"I'm Tracy Oshkosh!" the young woman said brightly. "I guess I beat the rush!"

"The rush?" The look of anticipation on her face spoke volumes. "Oh, did you think the grand opening was today? It's not until tomorrow. I'm the owner, Samantha Armstrong."

She dug out her cell and scrolled. "I was *sure* my boss said it was today. I would have been here this morning, only I overslept…"

My aunt and I exchanged glances.

I waited for her to stop scrolling but after thirty seconds of her head glued to her phone, I asked, "Who is your boss?"

"At the paper. I work at *Pulse on Palm Beach*."

I can't say I wasn't thrilled a paper wanted to cover my grand opening. Too bad she was a day early.

"That's great, but like I said, it's not until tomorrow. I'm glad your boss knew about it, though."

Distracted, Tracy mumbled and studied her phone. "She says it's part of the job." A moment later, a look of surprise and disappointment crossed her face as she settled on something on her cell and stopped the frantic scrolling. "Oh." She peered up at me.

I raised my brows and tossed her a little smile because geez, I know *I* mess up sometimes.

"You're not opening until tomorrow," she said like she was telling me something I didn't know.

My smile broadened. I couldn't help it. She was sort of ... cute, in a ding-dong kind of way. "Yup."

Her eyes scanned the café, the door to the back room, and everything in between—the display case, espresso machine, colorful napkins, stainless steel trash can. She pressed her lips together like she was mad at herself maybe, then shrugged, smiled and bopped out the door, her brunette ponytail swinging on her perky little head.

"Was that strange?" I asked my aunt.

Before she had time to answer, I moseyed over to the front door to lock it. Whitney Goodwin, the owner of the new pastry shop two doors down shoved Tracy out of her way and beamed at me through the glass door. If I didn't want to create an enemy, I had to welcome her inside.

Whitney sailed in, scanned the café, and glanced at Aunt Mary. Her beam faltered into something between a sneer and a smile. I had only spoken with her one time and honestly, I was so busy petting her dog I didn't take much notice of her face. She was much prettier than I remembered, as blonde as I was brunette. Taller, too.

"Hi, Whitney. How's it going over at Patisserie?"

"Oh, business is booming, you know." She smiled ever so slightly at Aunt Mary. "And who is this?"

"I'm sorry. This is Mary Price, my aunt. Aunt Mary, this is Whitney Goodwin. She's the new owner of Patisserie of Palm Beach."

"Oh, I know your parents," my aunt said.

"Small world," Whitney said with a smile and turned to me. "I thought you might want to know ... I just heard a rumor that not everyone is happy to have a dog bakery here."

I felt my eyebrows rise to my hairline. "Here? In Palm Beach?"

"Yes. More precisely, on Worth Avenue." She shrugged like it meant nothing but her smile made it look like she had found a hundred-dollar bill in her pocket. *If she thinks she's going to scare me away, she can say sayonara and sail right back out my front door the same way she sailed in.*

"Where did you hear that?" I asked, all sweet-like. No need to become arch-enemies with the woman.

She waved her hand and chortled like she meant it all in good fun. "Oh, don't worry about it. It's not like you can pack up all your ..." She swept Canine Confections with her eyes. "Your ... dog bowls? I don't know, whatever it is you have here ... and close up shop." She tilted her head and smiled.

I tilted my head and smiled right back. "Well, I *can* close shop before I even open. But I won't." Big smile. I learned back in junior high, don't let the mean-spirited girls run roughshod over you.

She looked at me, bewildered, and huffed something about people not knowing who they're talking to. Then, she turned on her heel and stormed out the door.

"Great," I said to Aunt Mary. "I can already see that running a business two doors away from Whitney will be like a daily dose of prune juice."

I hate prune juice.

CHAPTER TWO

I woke up the following morning before dawn with a spring in my step. Okay, maybe not a spring. A steady prance.

It was the grand opening day of Canine Confections, the biggest accomplishment in my life so far. And I'm no dummy, I knew it wasn't *my* accomplishment as much as the fact I had a generous aunt who could afford to give me a shot at my dream. A month ago, Aunt Mary had had a car accident that required knee surgery, crutches, and somebody to look in on her at home. She could certainly afford at-home care, but she only wanted family. Keeping a close eye on her wasn't as easy as it sounds when the place I'd moved into was a big freaking mansion. Technically, I moved into the cottage on her estate next to the mansion. Or as I liked to refer to it, The Big House.

Aunt Mary's investment made Canine Confections' success only more important. Also, I reminded myself, I socked every extra penny into it that I had saved. If it failed, I didn't know what I would do. Run back to Sun Haven and my job at Debbie's Bakery with my tail tucked between my legs? Save up enough cash again to put a down payment on an apartment rental? At just above minimum wage, that would take me at least another five years. Plus, I would have to ask my mother to change the craft room back into my bedroom even though I was twenty-seven years old, and that wasn't going to happen. I'd rather live under a bridge. And I was not living under a bridge.

I ignored all of that and jumped in the shower, still enthralled with the rainfall showerhead and marble tub that made the rusty showerhead and chipped ceramic in Peter's bathroom look like a half-star motel. The bathrooms in the Big House were even grander, with jacuzzi tubs and heated towel racks. I knew this because I had helped my aunt take a shower the first couple of weeks I was here, until one evening she told me "enough was enough" and that I was making her feel like an invalid.

I dried myself off with a fluffy white towel, brushed my teeth with the regular toothbrush and the electric toothbrush for the extra zing, grabbed my paperwork I'd brought home the night before, and ran over to the Big House to check on her.

At that early hour, she was still asleep. I strolled over to her king-sized bed and watched her chest rise and fall, just to make sure. Next, I texted Alice to confirm she would be driving Aunt Mary to my grand opening, not that I thought my aunt should be out with her cane in what I hoped would be a crowd, but because I knew that if Alice *didn't* bring her, my aunt might hurt her knee driving herself over to Worth Avenue. Her physical therapist was very clear—Aunt Mary should work up slowly to bending her knee too frequently. That was why she was only supposed to do three reps at a time on the stationary bike rather than the four my aunt insisted upon because she wanted to get better "and fast." Patience doesn't run in our family.

Aunt Mary slept soundly while I watched over her, waiting for Alice's return text.

Within two minutes, Alice returned my text: You woke me up. Yes, I'll bring Mary.

Back at my cottage, I fiddled with my hair, poured piping-hot coffee into a mug and hurried out to my car. As I waited for the electronic gate to open out onto Ocean Avenue, I marveled that I lived on an estate across from the Atlantic Ocean. My aunt had begun keeping in touch more frequently after my uncle died a few years ago, so it wasn't a complete surprise when she offered me a place to live and the cash to open what she always knew was my dream job of a dog bakery. Aunt Mary thought the splashy Worth Avenue would be the perfect location when I explained I wanted a comfortable but sophisticated atmosphere. Her timing had been perfect, as if a metronome sat in her sixty-nine-year old tummy—and that's saying something, since her closest affinity to music was humming the theme song to *The Golden Girls.*

Right about the time I had walked in on my boyfriend and so-called best friend in the apartment Peter begged me to move into before he decided things were moving "too fast," I moved out of Peter's, quit my job at Debbie's Bakery and scampered up to Palm Beach quicker than a duck jumping into a puddle.

I held tight to my mug with my right hand as my left held the steering wheel, enjoying the wrapped-in-a-blanket feeling a to-go cup simply could not emulate. Due to the dark hour of five a.m., I couldn't *see* the ocean to my left, but I could hear its roar from my open window. I could also feel the humidity even though the sun wouldn't shine for another couple of hours. *Thank you, summertime in South Florida.*

By the time I made it over to Worth Avenue ten minutes later, my mug was empty and my body was in overdrive. The mayor of Palm Beach was going to cut the ribbon for my ribbon cutting ceremony. Sure, he cut one only a week ago for Whitney's Palm Beach Patisserie, but I was still excited. I parked in a primo spot directly in front of Canine Confections and scanned Worth as I exited my car. Nothing but a pair of headlights from a lone delivery truck at the other end of the avenue and one lone figure walking past the luxury linen store across the street.

I zipped up onto the sidewalk, pulled out the store key, and guessed at the keyhole since I couldn't see a thing. A moment later, *key* met *hole*. I smiled and opened the door wide as it would go.

"It's the big day!" I announced to my empty dog bakery.

Empty that is, except for the dead body lying on the floor.

CHAPTER THREE

My jaw dropped. I'd never seen a dead body before, except for Uncle Joseph's. Not even on a trip to the Big Apple where my mother freaked me out a little and made me call her every day on that trip. For the record, I was fine—not once was I mugged or murdered.

The dead stare of the woman and the wooden rolling pin lying on the floor by her head told me I didn't have to worry about rushing over and giving mouth-to-mouth.

I held tight to the keyring in my hand, like it was a life raft to normalcy. Then, I inched over for a closer look and gasped. The dead woman lying on my dog bakery floor with my wooden rolling pin next to her head was Whitney, the owner of Palm Beach Patisserie who had warned me that she heard a rumor my dog bakery was not welcome on Worth Avenue.

Pulling a small mirror from my purse, I knelt down and placed it in front of her mouth like I'd seen it done on TV. A shiver ran up my spine when no breath fogged it up. In the silence, I thought I heard Whitney breathing. I leaned over her face and examined it. Super pretty. Long, straight blond hair, blue eyes. Sure, the eyes were lifeless and staring up at the ceiling, but they were pretty. I like to find the positive. Sue me.

Her pink lipstick was only smudged a little and her nostrils didn't budge. Leaning back on my knees, I moved my eyes to her chest and waited for it to rise and fall. Nothing.

Yet I still heard somebody breathing. I was pretty sure at that point that I was imagining things, only the breathing was definitely getting louder. On the off-chance that I wasn't having a mental breakdown, I stood up and scanned the café for somebody else besides me who was alive.

That was when it occurred to me that it was probably the murderer. *Alive and here and watching me at this very moment!* I started to bolt out the front door onto Worth Avenue, when a sound came from the back room. I stopped and wheeled around. If I were in a horror movie, this would be the point where the audience moans at my stupidity for heading directly into the fray. But nothing should have been back there except for my desk, a walk-in refrigerator, and a walk-in supply closet. I looked at Whitney on my floor. If whoever murdered her ran out the back door, it would make it that much harder for the police to find them. Of course, the murderer could kill me too and leave, and that wouldn't help the police. Oh, and I'd be dead.

Right in the middle of the argument I was having with myself, the loud breathing from the back room increased in volume. Then, somebody cried. Or whined. I looked out the front window, wishing for company, but all I could make out in the dark was the outline of my car and a jogger across the street. The high-pitched whine grew louder. I couldn't leave someone lying there suffering. *Suppose the murderer left another body in my backroom, someone who was not yet dead?* I pressed 911 on my cell, gave them Canine Confections' address, and grabbed a knife off the counter behind the display case before I lost my nerve. Slowly, I made my way to the door of the back room. I kept my eye on the knob, relieved that it wasn't a swinging door that could smack me in the face if someone decided to ram through it.

The knob remained still. The quick exhalations of breath from the back continued. So did the whine.

I inhaled deeply, held up the knife like I knew how to use it for something other than slicing snippets of butter into my Pupcake Frosting recipe, and opened the door to the back room.

The face that greeted me couldn't have taken me more by surprise.

CHAPTER FOUR

"Sweet Pea!" I called out to the black dog with white paws staring at me. Her ears were flattened in fear, thanks to my abrupt entrance. "Did somebody lock you back here?"

Sweet Pea was Whitney's new dog. I had met her briefly one day in the middle of a particularly rushed afternoon when Whitney and I were zipping past each other on the sidewalk. Whitney told me that she had recently adopted her from the local shelter. She was cute as could be. A mutt, I thought. Mixture of black Labrador and somebody smaller. Cocker spaniel, maybe. Currently with a pink leash dangling from her jeweled collar.

Once Sweet Pea recognized me, her ears relaxed and her mouth opened slightly. I smiled and tilted my head at her cute little face, and her tail tentatively untucked from between her legs.

"Come here, little girl, it's okay," I said and gently tapped my hand to my thigh in a beckon.

She stared up at me. I fought the impulse to rush over and hug the furball, because I didn't want to scare her. Also, I wasn't one-hundred percent sure the murderer was gone.

Quietly, I said, "Hold on a sec," held the knife up in the air and listened at the doors to the walk-in refrigerator and supply closet. I couldn't hear anything over the refrigerator hum and my ragged breath. Sweet Pea's mouth was closed shut as she observed my every move. My eyes fell on the door that led to my patio and back alley. The lock was broken and lying askew. It answered my question of how Whitney, Sweet Pea and the killer gained access to my dog bakery, but the question was *why*?

The broken lock meant I couldn't secure Canine Confections. Somebody could return. And I still hadn't checked *inside* the two walk-ins to see if the murderer left a body in them, someone who needed help.

Sweet Pea softly began whining again and padded to the door that led to the front of Confections.

"I'm not sure that's a good idea." The last thing I wanted was for the dog to see her owner lying dead on the floor. I wished I could ask Sweet Pea what *she* wanted. I studied her hairy black face. Her brow wrinkled above her concerned brown eyes. She whined and scratched the door one time with her paw to let me know she wanted access to the front.

I removed her leash and opened the door between front and back.

Sweet Pea stepped into the cafe and stopped when her gaze met Whitney's body lying next to the display case. Her nose wriggled, she let out a tiny whine, then she tucked her tail between her legs and flattened her ears to her head.

"It's okay," I said softly.

A glance up at me and a furrowed brow told me she questioned my assessment of the situation. Slowly, she padded over to Whitney. She sniffed her owner's head, then retreated and looked up at me with baleful eyes.

"I'm sorry, baby. I know," I cooed. I laid the knife and leash down on a table, kneeled on my glossy floor and opened my arms to her. The furry black mutt slowly came over and let me hug her. "I'm so sorry," I whispered, grateful she had only known Whitney for a short time and hopefully wouldn't grieve too long.

She leaned her head into my chest and let me rub her ears and after a minute, her body relaxed and I even got a tail-wag. Then, effusive licks. I laughed and checked her collar. Nothing but her name. I checked under the hood to make sure I had my facts straight and that she was a girl. *Yup.*

"Let's wait outside for the police." I grabbed her leash off the table, clasped it onto her collar, and led her out to the dark sidewalk in front of Canine Confections. I checked my cell. Not even six a.m. yet. The mayor was due to arrive in three hours.

I sat on the concrete bench in front of Confections and left a message on the mayor's voicemail that my grand opening was called off due to an incident at my dog bakery. I pressed "end" on my cell, my eyes and ears peeled for movement. The ants in my pants wouldn't stop running up and down my legs, so I got up from the bench and began pacing the sidewalk with Sweet Pea, first past the art gallery next door and Whitney's Patisserie next door to *that*, then back past Confections, Rare Books and Stamps next door, and the pet store next to *him*. I almost made it to Jimmy Choo but a police car pulled up in front of Confections, so Sweet Pea and I hurried back.

A police officer with a serious expression on his tanned face met us under the canopy that shades the large display window of Canine Confections.

"Don't police officers usually come in twos?" I asked. "Like Twinkies?"

His eyes flashed up to mine. "Palm Beach only has one responding officer. You the one who called in?"

"Yes." *And I'm freaking out right now.*

He pulled out a pad, but not before Sweet Pea nuzzled his hand. "Friendly. Name?"

"Sweet Pea," I answered and pressed my hand to my leg to stop the nervous jiggle.

He blinked at me. "Your name is Sweet Pea?"

"Oh. No. I'm Samantha Armstrong. Sorry, I'm a little … thrown."

He steadied his gaze past the fancy pink font of Canine Confections on the window and into my dog bakery. "You said she's dead, right?"

"Well, yeah, but maybe you want to make sure?"

He looked at me and I finally understood the phrase *if looks could kill.*

Headlights beamed towards us not a second later. An ambulance screeched to a halt and parked behind the squad car. I leaned on the palm tree next to me as though it would give me support.

The officer asked me a few rudimentary questions and checked out my license. By the time he was finished, a gentleman in his sixties wearing a pastel pink shirt lumbered over, and the officer took off.

"I'm Detective Trumble," he said. Sweet Pea licked his hand. The detective tapped the top of her head with one hand and stuck a Tootsie Pop into his mouth with the other. The disparity between his gruff manner, and pink shirt and lollipop threw me off a little, as though all could not co-exist in one detective. Trumble observed the EMTs inside Confections with Whitney. At least half an hour had passed since I made my calls, and the EMTs had been checking on Whitney for the past ten minutes. Since they weren't rushing out of here with her on a stretcher, I knew it meant I had been right that she was dead.

Distractedly, I massaged Sweet Pea's ears while I waited for the detective to read through my answers to the officer's questions. In the next instant, a car pulled up. Aunt Mary threw open the passenger door, while Alice gave her a dirty look from behind the wheel.

"Samantha!" my aunt cried.

"What are you doing here?" I rushed over to help her with her cane. Sweet Pea nuzzled her hand while Alice rounded the car.

"I heard something happened," she said anxiously as she took in Detective Trumble and the EMTs.

"How would you hear that already?"

Alice's long red hair draped in front of her face as she busied herself with accepting Sweet Pea's kisses. When Aunt Mary's eyes fell on her, the personal assistant must have felt our stares because she said, "You wouldn't believe how much people gossip in this town."

My aunt's cane caught on something. She stumbled forward but I gripped her arm and held her steady while Alice smiled at an officer zipping past.

"You're supposed to be resting," I said to my aunt.

"I wanted to make sure you were alright."

"And you couldn't call?"

"It's not the same as seeing you for myself." She stepped forward slowly towards the bench. "And I couldn't wait to hear from you."

I settled her onto the bench while Trumble watched, a frown in the folds of his face. "Your impatience is going to be the death of me."

She chortled softly. "*My* impatience?" Aunt Mary reached down for Sweet Pea's soft muzzle. "Who is this?"

"The dead woman's dog," I said quietly. "So how exactly did Alice hear about this already?"

Aunt Mary massaged Sweet Pea's neck and glanced at her assistant. "She has a friend who works at the mayor's office."

Her face grew serious at the EMTs lifting Whitney's body onto a gurney inside Confections. "What happened?"

"I found Whitney Goodwin lying on my floor."

"Oh no!" she exclaimed. "And we just saw her last night!"

Detective Trumble, who had been taking this all in, lifted his eyebrows. His sharp eyes moved from me to my aunt to Alice and back to me. "You two just showed up for the first time this morning, correct?" he asked Aunt Mary and Alice.

"Yes," they said in unison.

He nodded and wrote something on his notepad, then turned around when a couple of officers began wrapping yellow crime scene tape around my dog bakery.

"I have a few questions to finish up with you," he said to me.

Aunt Mary looked at me anxiously. Trumble nodded at her and I could swear her face turned pink.

"Do you want to wait here while I talk to the detective, or do you want to go home and I'll call you later?" I asked her.

"Of course I want to wait here," she said and turned to Alice. "I'll call you in a little while to pick me."

Alice shrugged, nodded and zipped back to the car without so much as a concerned backward glance.

Trumble stuck a Tootsie Pop into his mouth, where it bulged his cheek out like a small bouncy-ball. "I could talk to you in the car if you want more privacy but …" He looked down at Miss Furry Black Butt.

"I'm fine here," I said and noted that, aside from my aunt, no one except the crime scene guys were near us. I hadn't seen anyone since the morning jogger and pedestrian walking across the street. "Oh!"

"Yes?" he said, eyebrows shooting up his forehead as he led me a few steps out of my aunt's earshot.

"I just thought of something! I saw somebody walk past earlier this morning and then a little while later somebody jogged past."

He scribbled on his notepad. "Same person?"

"I have no idea. It was too dark to see."

"Similar height, weight? Male, female?"

I rummaged through my brain and came up almost empty. "Medium height? Moderate frame." I checked on my aunt, who was keeping her eyes glued on me and the detective.

"Okay, let's move on for now." He scanned his notes. "You saw the victim last night?"

"Victim? Oh, Whitney. Yeah, she came into Confections to let me know there's a rumor that people don't want a dog bakery here."

His eyes glazed over for a moment, taking that in. "How did you respond?"

"I let her know I wasn't going to be scared away."

He waited a moment. "You told the responding officer that you found her on the floor. Anything else you want to add?"

"Not really."

I couldn't seem to take my eyes off of the EMTs packaging Whitney up like a morbid Christmas present. Scurrying around them, women and men busied themselves lifting fingerprints, snapping pictures, and jotting notes.

"Whitney's pastry shop is for people while yours is for ..." he cast his eyes down at Sweet Pea.

"Dogs. Yes."

Scribble, scribble.

I didn't want to ask but I went ahead anyway. "She was killed, right? I mean, it's not like she hit herself over the head with a rolling pin."

"I don't know anything now. All we know is it's a suspicious death."

What is he saying? She might have come to borrow a rolling pin and died of a heart attack? I chewed my lip.

Trumble asked, "Do you have any idea who would want to hurt her?"

"I was wondering the same thing. I just moved here a month ago so I don't know too many people."

He held his pen mid-air. "To Palm Beach?"

"Yes. Into a cottage at Whitehall, my aunt's estate." I pointed vaguely at Aunt Mary.

The EMTs covered Whitney's face with a sheet. Bile started to rise up my throat.

"Are you alright?" Trumble asked.

"That's my rolling pin next to her head."

"I was going to ask you about that."

"About my rolling pin?"

"Right."

"What do you want me to say? I probably won't use it anymore …" Dawn had broken a while ago but rather than cheer up the crime scene, it only brought it to harsh clarity. Cars began to show on Worth

Avenue. "That's how she was killed, right? Somebody hit her over the head with it?"

"How did you feel about a bakery being only two doors away from yours?" he asked, ignoring my question.

"I felt fine. Mine is for dogs."

He nodded and scribbled on his pad.

A car squealed into a parking spot, and a cameraman and a reporter rushed up. The officers running the crime scene tape held their arms up to hold them back. The cameraman pointed his camera into Confections' display window. In a microsecond, the reporter next to him switched her expression from frantic to sincere, as she directed her gaze into the camera. "We're here from *Pulse on Palm Beach* at Canine Confections in the normally quiet luxury shopping district of Worth Avenue."

Pulse on Palm Beach. That was the same paper that young woman from yesterday was from ...

The reporter leveled the microphone at the officer with the crime scene tape in his hand. "Sources have told us that Whitney Goodwin has been murdered. Can you confirm?"

The officer exchanged a quick glance with Trumble, who glared. "Let us do our job," the officer said.

The reporter said quietly to the cameraman, "We're sure she was murdered, right?"

He shrugged and smirked as if to say, "Does it really matter?" and lifted the camera to his shoulder again.

The reporter directed her gaze into the lens. "We'll continue to keep you updated with the latest news on the murder of one of our own right here at Canine Confections on Worth Avenue. I'm Donna Richards from *Pulse on Palm Beach.*"

It was exactly as I had hoped my grand opening would go.

CHAPTER FIVE

The shops on Worth Avenue are a Palm Beach favorite with locals as well as visitors and this morning it was bustling with looky-loos who had already heard the news about Whitney. Detective Trumble left me and Sweet Pea while he checked on things inside. I started over to my aunt, holding Sweet Pea close to keep her from licking every officer and onlooker we walked past.

"You must be some watchdog," I said to her after she sniffed and tried to reach out to another person walking by.

She replied with a happy grin.

I paused on the way to the bench to hear what the cameraman and reporter had to say. I only caught bits and pieces.

"She was supposed to be next in line," the reporter said.

"That's how the rich stay rich," the cameraman answered with a chuckle, camera on his shoulder at the ready.

I had no idea what they were talking about.

Aunt Mary's face was flushed and pinched. I sat next to her and tried to lighten the mood. "What's up with you and Kojak?"

First, a look of surprise from Aunt Mary, then a demure smile. "I don't know what you're talking about."

Her reaction only made me more certain. "So, there *is* something going on between you two."

"How do you know who Kojak is?"

"Cozi TV," I answered. "Well? Tell me. God knows *my* love life is at a boring standstill right now."

"He's six years younger than me."

"So? You're a spry sixty-nine. Women date younger men all the time." Maybe not *all* the time. But every blue moon, at least.

Aunt Mary laid the cane at her side and stretched her leg out from the bench. She wore no bandage on her knee.

"It seems to be healing pretty well," I noted.

"Yes."

I waited.

"That wasn't meant to get us off the subject. What's up with you and the detective?"

She shrugged a delicate shoulder. "After Uncle Joseph died, I had a couple of incidents at the house."

"In your mansion?"

She scoffed. "Mansion."

"That's what it is, isn't it? What kind of incidents?"

"The security alarm went off a few times. I thought somebody was trying to break through the electronic gate, so Bruce showed up each time to check on it for me."

"Bruce. That's Trumble's first name?"

She nodded. "It turned out I was putting in the wrong code in the evenings. Since Uncle Joseph and I didn't like having live-in staff to do things like that, and since your uncle was very old-fashioned and thought that fell under the things a man does, I had no idea." She chuckled. "Just like he thought it was the man's job to hire someone to take care of the money and investments. He left me in the dark about it and I'm embarrassed to say, I let him."

I reached over and pressed my hand to hers.

She said, "It's a whole new world out there from when I was growing up. Women don't wait for their husbands to allow them to do things anymore." She brought her leg back in and bent it at the knee but winced.

I was no authority on high finances. My current predicament had me in a make-it-or-break it scenario.

Sweet Pea panted and gazed up at my aunt with concern. I would interrogate my aunt later, I thought.

People began wandering up to the crime scene tape. "Do you feel better now that you saw me? Can we get you home so you can ice your knee?"

"I'll call Alice. But I hate to leave you like this."

"I'm alright. You need to stop worrying."

"You should talk." Aunt Mary called Alice and we massaged Sweet Pea's head and ears until the personal assistant wheeled up to the curb.

Since Alice sat behind the wheel rather than run out to help, I held my aunt's elbow and guided her over to the passenger seat, settling her cane next to her.

Sweet Pea thought she was going in the car and started to climb in too.

"You're staying here with me," I told her. She responded with a lick to my hand.

I shut Aunt Mary's door and gave her a quick peck on the cheek. "Call me if you need anything."

I barely had time to move out of the way before Alice peeled away from the curb and down Worth Avenue.

Trumble exited Confections and said to the cameraman and reporter, "Give us some room here, would you?"

The cameraman smiled, happy, I assume, to have gotten that last bit of sass on live camera.

"We have to call Animal Control for the dog," Trumble said to the officer at his side while he unwrapped another chocolate Tootsie Pop.

"No!" I shouted and joined him up near the yellow tape. I forced myself to act calm in front of the guy with a gun and lowered my voice. "I'll be responsible for her."

"Fine. Save us the trouble."

The officer said something into his ear.

"Don't go far," Trumble said to me and started to head inside.

"I was supposed to open today," I called after him and pointed to the sign in the window. From the look he threw my way, I figured that was off the table.

Through the large display window of Canine Confections, the officers meticulously picked up fingerprints. That was all well and good, but I knew from *Forensic Files* that would work only if the murderer's prints were already in the system from a previous crime. No one seemed too concerned about cleaning up the powder or righting my overturned chairs, and that was nothing compared to poor Whitney being murdered. Thank goodness for the Florida sun gleaming onto the front window … it added a touch of cheer.

So did the man strolling up to me and Sweet Pea at the bench. Mr. Sexy Stubble, the guy walking past Canine Confections yesterday when I was inside with Aunt Mary. Only this time he was walking towards me with three Starbucks coffee cups in his hands.

In an instant, Sweet Pea stood up, wagged her tail, and reached up to his wrist with her long, wet tongue.

"Bad morning?" he asked me.

My mouth fell open in surprise, but I knew better than to look a gift horse in his very attractive mouth. "You might say that."

"I thought you might be able to use this." He handed me one of the cups, set one on the ledge of the building and removed the lid off the third. "Is she allowed?" he asked and tilted the cup to show me the whipped cream inside.

"Sure," I said. "Thanks."

He scratched the top of Sweet Pea's head and held the cup in place while she lapped up the cream in ten seconds flat. Sexy Stubble threw the cup into the trash bin, returned to us, and lifted the other cup from the ledge. He gestured to the inside of Confections. "That an espresso machine I see in the back?" He leaned against the building all cool-like, one leg bent at the knee, foot pressed to the building's side.

I twisted around and looked past the fingerprint guys to the espresso machine behind the display counter. "Good eyes. Yup."

He rubbed underneath Sweet Pea's chin. "She looks like the dog Whitney just adopted. She owns the pastry shop a couple of doors d—" Frown lines creased his forehead. "Wait a minute ... what happened here?"

"I found her lying on the floor when I got here this morning." I said this with all the feeling of a robot. Somehow, I felt removed from the situation. "I'm sorry. I guess you two were friends."

"We went to school together."

He looked upset but not stricken. Maybe he wasn't upset about the death of someone he knew, maybe that was why he didn't shed any tears. Or maybe he was a cold-blooded killer.

"Sorry for your loss," I said, trying to keep my voice steady. I found comfort in the officers on the other side of the window. "Thanks for the coffee and whipped cream but I don't even know your name."

He grinned. "Rick Newman. I own Sophisticated Pet two doors down."

"Which means we're neighbors trying to sell to the same customers," I said all friendly-like.

"No," he said. "I sell collars, leashes, raincoats …"

"Raincoats?"

"Yeah," he said. "Mostly for the little ones. They get uncomfortably wet if it's raining. Not like this big girl," he said and leaned forward to run a hand across Sweet Pea's back. "What would you say she is, about thirty-five pounds?"

"Something like that. She doesn't seem big to me." Growing up, my parents only had dogs sixty-five pounds and up.

"Put her up next to a chihuahua, she'd look like a giant!" He rested his foot against the building again and made small talk. "Yeah, I sell a few dog snacks, too."

I nodded. My antennae went up for the second time in a matter of minutes. *Current pet store owner wants to run me out of business before I'm even open, throws a dead body on my floor …*

He paused before taking a sip from his cardboard cup. "What happened? You got pale all of a sudden."

I shrugged. "Nothing."

"Are you afraid I'm going to run you out of business with the three snacks that I sell?" he asked with a twinkle in his blue eyes.

"I'm good," I said and smiled.

No sense sharing my thoughts with him. Let him think I don't know how to put two and two together.

CHAPTER SIX

About the time I was freaking myself out thinking Sexy Stubble from Sophisticated Pet was a murderer, Tracy, the young woman from the day before bounded over.

"I missed the boat," she said to me with a nod to Rick. "I heard a couple of the others from *Pulse* were here already." She bent down, rubbed Sweet Pea's head and accepted kisses from the precious pup with the delighted giggle of a child.

Rick leaned over and murmured into my ear. "Careful. *Pulse* is the local *National Enquirer*," he said and walked away.

I turned my attention to Tracy, still leaning over and petting Sweet Pea. "I'm sort of in the middle of something." I gestured at the remaining officers inside Confections.

"I know," she said, nodding. "Whitney was murdered."

"We don't know that. Wait, how did you ..." I started to ask until I remembered the Palm Beach gossip train.

"It's a small town," she answered. "Do you mind if I ask you a few questions?"

Honestly, what harm could it do at this point? "Go ahead."

"This is your bakery, right?" she asked, pointing up at the fancy script on the glass window under the canopy. "You own it?"

"Yup."

"And it's called Canine Confections."

Nothing gets past her. "Right."

Two little lines creased between her eyebrows. Her lips pressed together.

I braced myself.

"So," she said. "Do you have any jelly donuts?"

"No."

She peered up at me with alarm. "I wonder if maybe it'd be a good idea? I think they're everybody's favorite, right?"

Her concern was … sweet. Or a little scary. *She was kidding, right?*

I gestured to the pink script on my window. "*Canine* Confections. It's a bakery for dogs."

Relief flooded her face. "Oh, right! Thank goodness! I mean, for *your* sake."

I nodded and smiled at the young woman. "First story?"

She shook her head. "No. Why?"

I shrugged, not knowing what to say.

"I think maybe I'm just not that good at it." She drew out her cell phone. "I don't suppose you'll let me get a picture of you?"

Rick had warned me about her, but what exactly did I know about *him*?

"Why not?" I said.

"Really?" Tracy stuck her notepad in her pocket and held her cell phone up. "Alright, just pose right there in front of the name on the window. And ... smile! Or, no, don't smile but ... ready?"

She snapped a picture and thanked me, unlike the other photographer who didn't stop taking close-ups until Detective Trumble ran him away. A growing crowd on the avenue whispered among themselves and I threw Rick's caution to the wind. "Hey, Tracy. I'm hoping you'll hold off telling people what happened until we actually know for sure but ... do you want to hang around for a little while?"

Her eyes brightened. "Sure!"

The girl seemed so earnest. And Sweet Pea really liked her, though that wasn't saying much since she seemed to like everybody.

Trumble exited Confections. Sweet Pea licked his hand a few times like he was a long-lost friend.

"What's up?" I asked. Silly me, I thought I had an *in* with the guy now that I knew he and my aunt had a thing, not that I was at all clear what the *thing* was yet.

"What's up?" he retorted, sarcasm dripping from his voice. He pulled me aside, six feet away from prying ears. Sweet Pea happily walked down the sidewalk with us on her leash.

"The rolling pin," he said. "It's yours."

I waited for his point since we already had discussed this.

Trumble mouthed something about my baking tools but my head began to swim. Blackness started to wash up and over me. A moment later, it passed.

"You with me?" Trumble asked.

"Yes. Sorry. What was the last thing you said?"

"I said keep yourself available. This is going to be a while." He glanced down the sidewalk at Tracy. "And if I were you, I'd watch who I talked to."

"What do you mean?"

"It means be careful." He unwrapped a lollipop. I was beginning to think the suggestion of a Twelve-Step program might not be out of line.

"Unless this whole thing is on you," he said with a little smile.

He was kidding, right? Making a little joke on my behalf?

He strode off and back into Confections.

Tracy skipped over. "Everything okay?"

"Yeah." I stared into Confections.

"What did he say?"

Remembering his warning about who to trust, I asked, "Did you know Whitney?"

"We all went to school together."

"Who's *we all*?"

"Me, Whitney, Rick, Bethany. The people along this strip of Worth Avenue."

"What can you tell me about her?"

"Well, she's twenty-seven years old, like me."

I thought Tracy was younger. "I'm twenty-seven, too." Why I inserted myself into Tracy's answer, I don't know. Nerves?

"Where are you from?" she asked.

"Couple hours southwest. Back to Whitney. What else can you tell me?"

"She still lives with her parents on Ocean Boulevard. Well, lived, I guess," she added sadly.

Ocean Boulevard. *My* neighborhood now, though Ocean Boulevard is a long road.

"And?" I pressed.

Tracy searched on her cell phone, then showed me a grand mansion replete with a pool and an ocean view. "Here's her house."

"Mmmm. Cute."

"Oh look! There's a story about you already!" Tracy cried as she showed me her phone: "Dog Bakery Serves Dead Bodies with Their Dog Biscuits."

I took a quick look. The title tried for pithy but the contents of the story expounded on the morbid facts that a woman was hit over the head and killed with one of my rolling pins.

"And they managed to get this out in the world in record time," I moaned. If this was how quick the press would jump on my unfortunate bandwagon, next thing you know, somebody would be writing an article on how my dog bakery was a place for evil and should be avoided at all costs. I wished Aunt Mary was here. Or better, that I *wasn't*.

Tracy shoved her cell into her bag and gaped at Confections. "Do you think there was a struggle? I thought Whitney was just bopped on the head."

How did she even *know* that? Trumble warned me not to trust anyone. This girl was way too cavalier. She attended school with the victim and was using cutesie language like *bopped?*

I said, "Actually, we don't know that. Aside from the mussed hair, she looks like she just fell over." *Or maybe whoever killed Whitney is just trying to throw us off, make us think it was a last-minute fight instead of a pre-meditated murder.*

The bleak situation turned grim when a man and woman rushed forward. Whitney's parents, I assumed. Their faces were ashen as Trumble spoke quietly to them. Whitney's mother broke down sobbing, and they soon left. I couldn't imagine how they must have felt. With Sweet Pea at my feet, it occurred to me I needed to get her to them. She belonged to their daughter and would maybe provide some comfort. But it was the last thing I wanted to do.

Bethany from Gallery Bebe stood and stared from the patio of her art gallery. I was ready to ask Tracy about her when an officer began removing the crime scene tape and Trumble told me I could go back inside.

"I thought they kept the crime scene tape up longer," Tracy said.

"I wouldn't know."

I headed inside and called the locksmith. He assured me he would arrive within an hour. "I guess I better get this cleaned up," I said with some annoyance, which, how's *that* for being self-absorbed? Girl dies in my dog bakery and I'm perturbed because I have to clean up the mess.

"Want help?" Tracy asked.

"Don't you have someplace to be? Computer, typewriter, office?"

She lifted one bony shoulder and began tidying up. "I'm supposed to be *here*. Last week, *Pulse* gave me the assignment to cover your grand opening, not that they cared. They give the good stories to the other reporters." Her face drew up in alarm. "I'm sorry! Your dog bakery is a good story!" She looked around at the mess. "I mean, it is *now*. It was before too, when you were just a dog bakery instead of the murder site of a Palm Beach resident…" She heaved a big sigh.

I smiled at Tracy despite myself.

Tracy threw out some scraps of paper the crime scene team left behind. "Sometimes I think my boss gives me any old story just to keep me thinking I'm writing for the paper."

"Why would they do that?"

"My uncle got me the job when the Palm Beach *Post* turned me down. He's a lawyer and got my boss freed of slander charges way back when, so I guess she feels she owes it to him."

"I never thought of Palm Beach as such a small town. It seems like all the residents know each other."

She paused to pet Sweet Pea, then slid a chair under a café table. "I guess. Don't you know everybody in your hometown?"

I shoved Peter's face into a corner of my brain until I was ready to think about my old boyfriend without throwing something. "Not really. Only my family and people I went to school with, and the customers who used to come into Debbie's Bakery."

Tracy's face lit up. She pulled out her notepad and held her pen above it. "Mind if I ask you some more questions?"

I played nice, keeping Trumble's warning in mind. "Sure." If she asked something I didn't want to answer, I wouldn't. I steeled myself for her question.

She furrowed her brow and asked, "If you *did* open a bakery for humans, do you think you would sell jelly donuts?"

CHAPTER SEVEN

I began picking up the overturned chairs. "Is that the line of questioning you think you should be going down?"

"What do you mean?" She frowned and slid another chair under a table.

"Maybe you want to find out when I plan to open now that today was a bust? If I knew Whitney? You know, like that?" I grabbed a roll of paper towels from under the counter behind the display case.

"I assumed you knew her." Tracy scooped her ponytail back. "Palm Beach Patisserie is two doors away."

"Right."

"Which makes it look pretty fishy that she was killed in your bakery."

Dog bakery, I wanted to clarify. "Why is it fishy?"

She mumbled to herself over and over, "Fishy, fishy. Sure smells fishy." Louder, she said, "Where did that saying come from, you think?

Because fish smell bad? They probably don't smell bad when they're swimming in the water..."

"Tracy."

"What?"

I shook my head at her. "Can we stay focused, please? What are the people like around here?"

She thought about it. "They're nice."

"You don't think they'll blame me just because Whitney was found in my dog bakery, do you?"

"Well, *yeah.*"

"Seriously?"

"Wouldn't *you* assume it if somebody new moved to your town and one of the locals got murdered?"

I took a deep breath. "No! And by the way, how do you and everybody know anything? When I called the mayor's office to call off the ribbon-cutting ceremony, I didn't give any details."

"Somebody from that office must have called Donna," she said matter-of-factly.

"Donna the reporter," I confirmed.

"Yeah."

I wondered if it was the same someone who called Alice, who then told Aunt Mary. "I guess once Donna and the camera guy got here, the rolling pin and Whitney's dead body told them all they needed to know. It's kind of weird that Whitney opened her business only a week before me."

"Not really. The town has been working on making infrastructure improvements the last few years, so there are a lot of changes happening." Tracy darted around the café, picking up errant trash, slipping chairs under tables and generally, making herself extremely useful. "Anyway, Whitney would have opened sooner except there was a snag in the paperwork or something."

"What kind of snag?"

"Huh?"

"You said there was a snag with the paperwork. What kind of snag?" Honestly, talking to her was like pouring a tablespoon of molasses out of the jar for my Sweet Molasses Pupcakes recipe.

"Something about money, I think," she said vaguely.

"For somebody who doesn't know much, you sure know a lot," I said in a tone that meant business under the lightness.

Sweet Pea lolled her tongue at me. "It's okay, girl. I just have to see what Tracy knows."

Tracy gazed at me, gave an innocent shrug and heaven help me, I think it was sincere.

"What else do you know that might be interesting, Tracy?"

"The other reporters at *Pulse* never ask my opinion." She pressed her finger to her chin and looked up at the ceiling for answers. Then, she leaned back on a table and observed the room, though at the time I had no idea what was so fascinating about tables, chairs and a couple of pictures on the wall.

"Renting commercial space on Worth Avenue is really expensive," Tracy explained.

"You don't say?" I replied.

She frowned at me with a quiz on her face.

"I'm sorry," I said. "Go on. You were saying?"

"I'm not sure, but I heard that her parents gave her the money for the bakery."

"Pastry shop."

"Huh?" she asked.

"I think Patisserie is a more of a pastry shop, not a bakery."

"What's the difference?"

"Bakeries sell bread," I said. "If Whitney is from here in Palm Beach, didn't she have enough money of her own?"

"Well, I guess she needed to buy bowls and spoons and stuff ..." Her voice trailed off as she stood with her back to me and faced a photo of a dog with yellow frosting all over his gold, fuzzy muzzle.

My sense was Tracy was either hiding her smarts, very literal in answering a question, or in my dog bakery for another reason altogether.

"Tracy?" I asked in a low, serious tone.

"Samantha?" she answered in the same serious low tone.

"Let's take a step back. Have a seat." I motioned to a chair at one of the round tables.

After she sat down, I said, "Can I have your attention and ask a few questions?"

She stopped the silliness and sat straight in her seat, a woman who attended Etiquette School. Like, for *real*.

"How do you know about Whitney and her parents and their money?" When she didn't respond, I said, "Work with me, Tracy."

She shifted in her chair and straightened her back like a rod of steel ran up her spine. "I'm trying." She clasped her hands in her lap. "Okay. I went to school with Whitney but we were never buddy-buddy. She was more a party-type girl. She ran around with these kids who got a little wild. Sometimes they'd get into trouble and their parents would have to bail them out."

"You mean literally? Bail-out-of-jail trouble?"

"No. I don't think it ever got to that. Or maybe it would have, except, you know … the people who live here have a lot of pull, so their kids don't get in trouble that much."

"You mean because of their money and connections."

Tracy's face squiggled. "I guess. I never thought about it like that."

Maybe because you're one of them.

"Whitney was pretty nice," Tracy said. "I think mostly she just went along with what other people talked her into."

"She was a follower?"

"No," Tracy said, unclasping her hands and finagling with the placement of the elegant Michael Aram napkin holder so that it angled instead of stood in the center of the table. "Actually, she was the leader of her group. The one who the other girls wanted to be around."

"But you just said she followed others."

"Yes. No. I mean ... it's hard to explain. She was so popular because everybody wanted to be around her. But she was sort of, I don't know, insecure maybe? She followed when other people wanted to do something, like she was afraid they'd all turn on her."

"I thought you said you didn't know her that well."

Tracy got up and moved on to another table, placing the napkin holder in the same spot as the other one, off to the side a bit. "We all went to school together from Kindergarten on up. You get to know people that way, even if you don't hang around them." She stepped back and considered the napkin holder, then moved it an inch to the left. "Do you realize how much of our lives are spent in school? How many hours does it add up to, you think?"

Staying the course, I asked, "So you saw all this with your own eyes? It wasn't just high school gossip?"

"Yup."

"What about the last ten years? What has Whitney been up to lately?"

A stricken look crossed Tracy's face. "What is she *up* to? She's up to being *dead* ..."

"Before she got ... murdered." The word left a bad taste in my mouth. Metallic, maybe. Or like old cheese.

Before Tracy said another word, the landline rang from behind the counter. My first call. I jumped up and answered. "Canine Confections, where our top priority is spoiling your pooch!" It sounded fake and tinny now that I said it out loud.

Tracy glanced over at me on the phone, then stood six feet from the wall and stared at another framed photo. Two puppies playing with a big, red ball.

From the other end of the phone, Detective Trumble said, "Miss Armstrong? Looks like we need to ask you a few more questions."

CHAPTER EIGHT

The phone in my hand, Trumble at the other end, I bit my lip. I was pretty sure telling him I wasn't up to any more questions right now wouldn't go over too well. "Can you give me an hour until the locksmith comes so I can lock up?"

"If it's too inconvenient, I can come back your way."

"It's just ... okay, I'll be there in a few minutes."

"You're a peach," he said and hung up.

I steadied my eyes on Tracy staring at the puppy photo in the café and quickly googled *Tracy Oshkosh from Pulse of Palm Beach* to make sure she hadn't robbed any banks or wasn't on the short list for the FBI's latest serial killers or anything. Nothing much popped up except a few pictures of her with friends at a posh restaurant and an article she wrote on how Floridians can make snow from scratch (baking soda and shaving cream).

Tracy moved on from the photo, grabbed a broom and began sweeping. Her ponytail swung back and forth with each *swoosh* across the floor. I was about to ask her something I might regret. *She might even become my first friend in my new town.* Not counting Aunt Mary and Sweet Pea of course.

I put aside my cell phone. "Would you mind waiting for the locksmith while I go to the police station?" *What more could happen? Another dead body? The cash register was empty, so that wasn't a concern.*

"Everything okay?" she asked.

"I think they just have more questions. No big deal."

"It's probably Trumble," she said and laughed. "He's known for pink shirts and asking a million questions."

"Right. And you know that because everybody knows everybody around here."

She shrugged. "Sort of."

Her vagueness was getting on my nerves, but that could have been because I'd been on edge ever since finding Whitney's body. I guess I led a sheltered life, if you call never finding a dead body lying around a sheltered life.

"It's no problem," Tracy said. "I'll tidy up the display case."

Tidy it up? I spent an hour yesterday arranging the Peanut Butter Delights and Puptail Pops.

I gathered up my purse, cell phone and Sweet Pea. I may trust my empty cash register with Tracy, but I wasn't about to trust my dog with her.

Amy Hueston | 57

"You're not leaving Sweet Pea with me?"

I didn't want to hurt Tracy's feelings but ... "No. Let the locksmith in obviously, but if anyone passes by or wants to come in, tell them we're closed. Leave the Closed sign on the door. And don't tell them about the murder." As if everyone in Palm Beach didn't already know.

Out on the sidewalk in front of Confections, I glanced over at Gallery Bebe. Martha, the woman who worked for Whitney at Patisserie, was sitting at a small table with Bethany. I smiled but they didn't smile back. I didn't hold it against them—it was a sad day.

Sweet Pea immediately jumped in to the car, which told me that the car represented more than only trips to the vet's office. Whitney and maybe her previous owner must have brought her on car rides to fun places. I remembered that of *course* Whitney brought her to fun places. Hadn't Rick recognized her from strolling around Worth Avenue? "I wish I knew more about your background. Maybe I'll call the shelter and ask them about you." *And maybe they'd drop a hint about Whitney, too.*

We skedaddled over to South County Road and arrived at the police station five minutes later, then checked in with the front desk. It was an excellent thing that they didn't mind a dog in their precinct, because I'm embarrassed to say that it hadn't occurred to me before then to ask if she'd be allowed.

Before I knew it, we were sitting in front of Detective Trumble's desk and I was tilting my head sideways to read the names of the operas on his DVD collection. The detective must be a Mozart fan, I thought. *The Marriage of Figaro* stood side by side with *The Magic Flute*.

Sweet Pea gave Trumble a kiss hello, then settled at my feet.

"Why did you move here?" he asked.

I would think he knew the answer if he and Aunt Mary were cozy as I assumed. "My aunt had a car accident and didn't want to hire a private nurse. She said she doesn't need a stranger to remind her to keep an ice pack on her knee." Okay, I did a little more than that, helped her with meals, in the bath the first few weeks …

The corners of Trumble's mouth curled up into an almost-smile. He bit his lip, blinked, and raised his brows at me. "You just dropped everything wherever you used to live and came here to help your aunt?"

I was too mortified to admit that my loser boyfriend and the woman who I thought was my friend snoodled up together and twisted my heart. And that I had procrastinated opening my own dog bakery for reasons I preferred not to share with the detective. "My aunt offered to help me open Canine Confections." Aunt Mary and I had an arrangement where she would profit by Confections' success. It was the only way I'd accept her generosity—which meant it *had* to succeed.

"Generous of her." Trumble scribbled on his notepad. "She lost her husband a few years ago."

"And she and my uncle never had any kids so I was the only family member available to move in and help her." A jar of chocolate Tootsie Pops stood on the corner of his desk. "What do you do with all the other flavors? Hand them out to the police officers on the other side of this door?" I asked, truly curious.

"You could have opened a dog bakery someplace else before now."

Still ignoring my questions, then. I side-stepped his question by disclosing only part of the truth, in loyalty to my parents' personal business. "The kind of dog bakery I want fits perfectly on Worth Avenue. Cozy but elegant. Not kitschy or cute."

"What's wrong with kitschy and cute?"

To the man who was neither kitschy *nor* cute I said, "Nothing. It's just not what I imagined."

"How much research did you do about other pet businesses before you moved here?"

I shifted in my chair. *What was he getting at? And why did he call me in?*

Sweet Pea moved from one haunch to the other at my feet as if she could sense my change in energy.

"I knew there was a pet store and no other dog bakeries," I answered. "If you don't mind my asking, what does all this have to do with Whitney?"

"Did you *know* about her bakery before you decided to open yours?"

"Mine is for dogs. Why do people keep forgetting that?"

"What people?"

I thought of Tracy and didn't mention her. He had already warned me of her, no need to dig *that* grave any deeper.

"I just meant … nothing."

He gazed at me with the tenaciousness of a dog gnawing a new bone. "Did you know about Patisserie or not?" Trumble asked all friendly-like before reaching for a lolly.

"Everything happened in a hurry, but yes. Does that matter?"

He shrugged his shoulders like his guess was as good as mine.

"This might be important," I said.

Interested, he twisted the tiny cardboard stick back and forth between thumb and forefinger and steadied his gaze on me without saying a word.

I asked, "Do you want me to take a polygraph?"

"Those things don't work," he said and unwrapped the Tootsie Pop.

Sweet Pea lifted her head at the crackling of the detective's candy wrapper.

"You can't have the tootsie roll inside," I said to her.

"Maybe I can rustle something up." Trumble pressed the intercom on his desk. "Bring me the dog treats."

"You keep dog treats at the police station? That's nice."

A knock sounded on the door. Sweet Pea jumped up.

"She's a friendly one," the officer said as Sweet Pea nuzzled his hand on the way to dropping the box of treats on Trumble's desk.

The detective exchanged a brief glance with the officer, who petted Sweet Pea's head one more time before he left.

She rounded his desk and opened her mouth for a treat.

After the second treat, I said, "That's enough for now, Sweet Pea."

Trumble wiped his hands on a tissue from the box on his desk and rolled up his pastel shirt sleeves.

"Whitney was killed, right?" I asked. "She didn't just die from a heart attack or anything?"

When the detective didn't answer, I said, "You can at least tell me if she was murdered, right?"

The detective folded his hands in front of him on his desk. "The problem I'm having is the rolling pin," Trumble said, back on focus and for some reason sharing his thoughts with me. Or the thoughts he wanted me to believe he was thinking to get me talking. "If somebody did want to kill Whitney, why would they use *your* rolling pin, unless it was you and it was an accident?"

"What kind of accident?"

"Maybe you and the girl got into an argument? Maybe you didn't like her telling you that your bakery wasn't welcome?" He leaned back in his chair and dreamed up other reasons I might have killed Whitney. "Maybe she threatened you and you had no choice but to protect yourself. Is that how it happened? I know some of these silver-spoons are hard to take, thinking the world owes them a favor…"

"No!" I said, startled at the panic in my voice. "Am I under arrest?"

"What are you talking about?"

I reached down and idly rubbed Sweet Pea's head. "*I* don't know how this works. Circumstantial evidence? You keep asking me about my rolling pin."

"You watch a lot of TV."

Anxious to get to the bottom of things, I said, "Why didn't the killer take the rolling pin? Weren't they afraid of leaving their fingerprints on it?"

I was beginning to get the impression that Trumble wasn't here to answer *my* questions. "I wouldn't be surprised if the residents blame you for this," he said. "People don't like dead bodies showing up next to their luxury stores."

"It's not like I carried a carcass on my back."

"There's already a news story on you." He picked up a remote on his desk and waved it at the television in the corner where ceiling met wall. A video of me, Sweet Pea, Trumble and the EMTs carrying the gurney with the headline: New Dog Bakery Owner Brings Grief to Palm Beach.

"I saw something like that online too," I said. The site Tracy had showed me.

"I'm sure it won't be the last. Reporters, huh?"

"Who would want to kill Whitney?"

Trumble didn't answer. Not even a *glimpse* into what he was thinking. Not an "I don't know," or a "That's what *we'd* like to know." For all I knew, he already had it figured out and was just putting the pieces into place.

To my horror, my eyes began to well up with tears like a big *girl*. I shook my head, grabbed a tissue off the desk and turned from him as I blew my nose and wiped my face. Sweet Pea got up and rubbed her muzzle into my lap. I took in a deep breath and rubbed her head. I couldn't look at Trumble. "Sorry. Nothing like this has ever happened to me before."

He leaned back in his chair again and steepled his fingertips under his chin as he studied me. "You've got a clean record."

"You checked my re ...?" Of *course* he checked my record. I gathered myself together. "I'm fine. What else?" I asked and met his stare.

"You left the Oshkosh girl alone when you came here."

"I know. Stupid, right?"

"Why?"

"Because I hardly know her," I answered. "It's stupid to leave someone I just me—"

"I mean why did you leave her?" he asked, leaning back in his chair and squinting at me.

My nerves moved from frayed to frazzled. "Because the back door was broken and the locksmith was coming, and you needed me to come here." I crossed one leg over the other and bobbed my foot up and down, a tic when I'm nervous or have something on my mind. After a second, I asked, "How do you know I left her?"

"You sure you and the girl didn't know each other before moving here?"

"Who? Me and Tracy? No."

He answered my questions with questions almost every time. It was really beginning to bug me.

"Anything else you want to tell me?" he asked.

"Not that I can think of."

"Well, if you *do* think of something, make sure to call right away. Meanwhile, we'll call you when we need you." He led me and Sweet Pea out of his office, through the police station's main office, and out the front door. The humidity slammed against my chest as soon as we hit the sun-splashed sidewalk. Trumble had said he wanted to know more about why the rolling pin was there, but that didn't make sense. He was sizing me up, feeling me out, seeing what I knew, where I flinched. *If I flinched.*

The sooner they found the killer, the sooner we could all move past this. I racked my brain for what I could do to speed things up. First up was finding out more about Whitney, though I didn't expect to get in to see the Goodwins that day since their daughter had just died.

Sweet Pea panted at my side. I needed to buy her a water bowl to keep in the car. Of course, she was Whitney's girl, not mine. Which meant, much as I didn't want to, I needed to find the Goodwins that day after all.

I opened the door for Sweet Pea, got in the driver's side, turned the air conditioning on full blast and called Canine Confections.

"I didn't get your cell number," I said to Tracy, the girl I had met only yesterday.

"Oh. Okay. It's—"

"No. I mean, yes, I'll get it but first … is everything okay there?" Trumble had put a bug in my head about her and now he had me not only *second*-guessing my choices, but third-and fourth-guessing.

"Perfect! The locksmith came and put a brand-new lock on the back door."

"Well, then you can leave. Thank you. No sense in you staying when we're not open."

"How would I lock up? The locksmith gave me new keys, but you need to get in. Unless you want me to hide it under one of your plants on the back patio …"

So she noticed the patio while the locksmith was there, I thought. *Oh well, she is a reporter.*

Whitney and her murderer had gained access to Confections through the back entrance where there was less of a chance of anyone seeing them. And that was *without* a key. "You better not hide the keys there. And do you mind if I leave you a little longer while I try to find where Whitney's parents live and find their phone number?" Not that I wanted to give Sweet Pea up, but what should I do? Wait to get attached and *then* have to give her to them?

From the other end of my cell, Tracy said, "I already showed you their house, remember? But their number … let me see … Pamela and Patrick Goodwin. It's a 917 number. Must be a cell. Ready?"

"How do you …? Never mind." I grabbed a pen and pad out of my purse, first time ever I had both handy when I needed them … the day was looking up already. "Go ahead."

Cold air blasted from the vents. Sweet Pea's fur blew backwards and her mouth hung open in a big, happy grin while I wrote it down. I hung up with Tracy, pulled out onto South County Road, then called the Goodwins right away, glancing at Sweet Pea and smiling at her lips flapping up and down from the current of the air conditioner.

A man answered with friendly professionalism, "Goodwin's residence. House Manager Robert Bradford." He gave me directions and ten minutes later, we were at the Goodwin's gate.

I pressed the buzzer, smiled into the small video camera on the pole, and felt like an idiot for smiling into their camera the day their daughter was killed. I waited while the gate opened—achingly slow—onto a driveway and lawn akin to an all-inclusive hotel. A spot you never want to leave ... trees hanging overhead, lush green plants, colorful flowers, and hedges that were probably pruned with bonsai clippers.

Sweet Pea started panting her dog-talk, that thing dogs do when they have something to say, and my heart fell. *This might be my last few minutes with her.* But what choice did I have? If Whitney's parents wanted her, she wasn't mine to keep. And how could I complain? Their daughter was dead.

I parked in the circular driveway and knocked on the big, brass door knocker, Sweet Pea at my side. A high-pitched bark sounded from inside the door. Sweet Pea whined with excitement.

A gentleman in a black and white uniform opened the door.

CHAPTER NINE

Before stepping inside the foyer, I asked the man who I assumed was Robert, "I heard a dog. I guess she and Sweet Pea are okay together?"

His face pinched. "It's fine," he said.

Sweet Pea tried to give him a lick but he shook his hand to nudge her away.

"Are you sure Whitney's parents are up to guests?" It struck me as strange that they were willing to meet with me when they just found out their daughter was killed.

Robert nodded and said curtly, "Yes."

What was I doing here? I asked myself anxiously as he led me to a grand library, the kind with floor-to-ceiling bookshelves. My answer: Telling Whitney's parents I had Sweet Pea and seeing if there was a morsel of information about who might have killed their daughter. I sat on the rich brocade of a Victorian chair. The little spiral-twist legs hardly looked strong enough to hold a child—looking at the rest of the furniture in the room, I suddenly had the urge to daintily cross my ankles.

Sweet Pea apparently had *no* such urge. She lay sprawled on the mahogany floor, her back legs straight out behind her in double-jointed splendor. Her ears twitched in alert-mode for the sharp bark we heard a minute earlier.

Whitney's mother entered the room with a glazed look in her eye and a tan chihuahua in her arms. "Sweet Pea!" she called.

Sweet Pea jumped up with her usual enthusiasm, but immediately held herself back from the growling and shivering chihuahua. *How had they managed to live under the same roof?*

"I'm Pamela Goodwin," the woman said and handed the chihuahua to Robert, who promptly left with the little pup. Her face was even more drawn than that morning, her eyes more dazed.

"Thank you for seeing me." *This woman's daughter died only hours ago.* My eyes burned. I blinked away the tears.

"I can use the distraction, to tell you the truth."

Now that the chihuahua was gone, Sweet Pea tugged to get closer to Pamela. I held her leash. "She wants to say hi."

Pamela stepped over, reached down and pat Sweet Pea's head, a fresh tear rolling down her cheek. She sat in a chair opposite of us three feet away.

The clock on the mantle struck nine thirty a.m. *Was it really only morning?* It felt much later. If I were back in Sun Haven, I'd be clocking in to my old job at Debbie's Bakery. My friends were showing up to their law firms or restaurants or accounting offices. My parents would be at their jobs if they weren't cruising in Belgium. But here *we* were, in the middle of a weekday morning, and Pamela Goodwin was home—and not only because her daughter had just died. I doubted that even if Whitney was fine, Pamela would be cleaning or doing laundry or mowing the lawn or cooking … these were things you hired *others* to do. Aunt Mary, for instance, had a chef and housekeeping staff come in three times a week.

Whitney's mother gazed past the bookshelf out the window to a patio overlooking the obligatory pool and tennis court on her Palm Beach estate. "Whitney only adopted Sweet Pea recently. She kept her in her wing of the house because of Baron."

Baron must be the chihuahua.

Still gazing out the window, Pamela said, "It was about the same time we bought Patisserie."

"I'm so sorry about your daughter."

She turned to meet my eyes, then shook her head and turned away. "I don't think it's sunk in yet."

"I think that's how it works."

After a moment of silence, she said, "The police said you were the one who found her."

"Yes."

She looked at me for more. *This* was why she had been willing for me to come over. But how many details did I want to give about how her daughter looked on the floor? *None,* that's how many.

Robert returned and stood as still as the bookcase next to him.

Pamela asked, "Would you like anything? Coffee?"

"Sweet Pea needs water, thank you."

Pamela nodded at Robert, who hurried off.

Even though I had a good, hard talk with myself on the way to Whitney's parents, my eyes felt hot. I'd only met Sweet Pea that morning but now that I had her, I didn't want to let her go.

My voice shook a little and boy did I feel like a jerk. "I guess … Sweet Pea is yours now."

"*We* can't take her!" Pamela cried. "Baron would never tolerate her."

"I can keep her?" I could hardly believe my ears.

"Or I'll have Robert bring her back to the shelter. Either way."

With perfect timing, Robert returned with a big bowl of fresh water. Sweet Pea drank a few sips and settled back at my feet.

Pamela observed the girl. "I always thought of shelter dogs as …" she stopped and eyed my seventy-five-dollar shoes. "It's not important. She's yours if you want her."

I swallowed hard to keep from bursting with a joyous *whoop!* and pressed my legs down with my hands to keep them from bouncing up and down.

Fully aware that it was so not my place to do this but wanting to get answers in a hurry, I racked my brain for questions. First up: "What shelter did Whitney get Sweet Pea from?" I asked Pamela. "I'll want to call them and make sure they know I'm keeping her. There's probably paperwork."

Pulled out of her haze, Pamela's eyes found mine. "Shelter? Oh, I don't know. Is there a Palm Beach Shelter? Robert can probably give you that information. Though I hate to let her go," she said, gazing down at Sweet Pea. "It would be like having a piece of Whitney with us."

No! I wanted to cry.

Right on cue, as if he heard from the other room, Baron made a beeline into the library directly for Sweet Pea. The little dog stopped a foot in front of the girl and began barking his little head off. Sweet Pea stood up, leaned her head slightly down for a whiff, and wiggled her nose at the noisy little thing.

Robert dashed into the room as Pamela rushed over and picked up Baron. She handed him over to Robert, who apologized and mumbled that he didn't realize the little dog had gotten out of the kitchen.

"It would take some getting used to but it's not impossible," I said. "They would have to get to know each other." *Why* was I *helping* her know how to keep Sweet Pea? Right. Because it was the right thing to do. I felt my eyes start to fill.

"Are you alright?" Pamela asked.

"Yes. I'm fine. It's just ..." I peered down at the girl, who was looking up at me with concern.

"Oh!" Pamela said. "*You* want her!"

"I'm sorry for being so selfish. Especially with all you must be going through …"

She smiled through tears. "I think Whitney would be happy her dog was living with someone who wanted her so much. And honestly, Baron is such a spoiled brat, it would take a long time before he would get used to sharing us." Pamela wiped her face with a tissue. Quietly, she said, "I'm afraid of the pain when the shock wears off. Whitney was our only child."

Why was she sharing such an intimate emotion with me?

Any words of comfort sounded hollow in my head so I didn't even try. If it weren't for her austere manner, I might have gone over and laid a hand on her shoulder.

I wanted to find out what I could about Whitney, but wasn't sure how to proceed. I wasn't known for my tact and didn't want to make Pamela feel any worse than she did, nor did I want to blow my chances for the future.

After a few minutes of chitchat, Pamela walked us to the foyer and Robert handed me Sweet Pea's dog bed and bowls. I worried for Pamela when reality set in.

I piled myself and Sweet Pea into the car. As soon as I wound our way out of the driveway and out the gate, I hugged my girl hard. "You're mine! I'm yours!" Tears flooded down my cheeks and I sobbed for a good two minutes. They were mostly happy tears but I had to admit, a lot of it might have been a release from the anguish of the morning. Sweet Pea seemed happy too, wagging her tail a mile a minute and sticking her head out the window after I was finally done squeezing her.

We tooled back to Canine Confections via Ocean Boulevard. I hoped Tracy was the reasonably capable adult I thought she was and didn't, oh, steal all my bowls or burn the place to the ground.

Ocean Boulevard—sometimes called A1A depending on where exactly you were on it—was the most scenic drive in South Florida. Truth be told, it's one of the most scenic drives in the Sunshine State. As you proceed south, the Atlantic Ocean is on your left, and on your right are the extravagant condominiums of the rich. I don't mean the *sorta* rich. I mean, the *really* rich. You may think someone who lives in what is a lot like an apartment may not have all that much money, but that's kind of like thinking an Olympic Bronze Medalist is *meh*.

I reached for my cell to call Aunt Mary but remembered that she told me she was going to ice her knee, take her pain meds and try to nap.

Sweet Pea stuck her head out the partly-open passenger window as we drove over to Worth Avenue. The garb on the passersby changed from swimsuits to linen as we approached it. I didn't know why Whitney opened a pastry shop when her life of privilege probably meant she could live off her trust fund. Except there's this rumor that the wealthy are people, just regular human beings. With the same wants and desires and idiosyncrasies as the rest of us.

It was almost eleven-thirty, but the closer I got to Worth Avenue, the more congested the traffic. Unlike other locations, Worth didn't have a standard lunch hour where the local office workers busied the streets so it made me wonder why the anomaly. By the time I found an empty parking space in front of Patisserie two doors down from Confections, it was almost noon.

A couple of women smiled as I clicked Sweet Pea's collar on to her leash and pulled out her bowls and doggy bed. Her bed would get more use at Confections, because who was I kidding? Sweet Pea would share mine at the cottage. She peered up at me with her big browns, inquiring about our next move.

With one hand holding the leash and the other arm wrapped around the dog bed and dishes, I was overloaded. The bed fell out of my arm onto the sidewalk, and the steel dishes clanged so loudly that shoppers stopped and stared. I was surprised Tracy didn't hear it from inside Confections and run over to help. Martha ran out of Patisserie. No sign of Bethany, however.

The clanking reverberated in my ears. Sweet Pea lowered her head an inch. Her tail shot between her legs. I kneeled down and massaged her velvet ears lying flat against her head. "Are you afraid of loud noises, honey?"

"I thought we had a Bell Tower to compete with the Clock Tower on the beach," Martha said. "I'm Martha Crenshaw. I work for Whitney." Her face fell. "Well, *worked*, I guess."

I rubbed one final time on top of the girl's head, stood up, and smiled at my neighbor. "I actually knew your name already, don't ask me how. It's been a whirlwind. I haven't had time to catch my breath."

"Did you know Whitney?"

"We've spoken a couple of times." No need to fill Martha in on Whitney's rude remark about my not being wanted on Worth Avenue. "I'm so sorry for your loss."

"Bethany told me Whitney was found next to your display case."

As I had learned, I was the talk of the town for all the wrong reasons. I'd left Tracy too long but wanted to know more about who was chatting up the bad news.

"Speak of the devil," Martha mused when the art gallery owner stepped out of the doorway of Gallery Bebe.

Bethany cast her eyes to Sweet Pea and didn't even pretend to smile. Swiftly, she turned on her shiny, spiky heel back in to the gallery.

"Figures," Martha said with a chortle.

A man and woman meandered over to Patisserie and opened the front door.

"Duty calls, I guess," she said sadly.

We said our good-byes, and Sweet Pea and I strolled past Gallery Bebe and into Canine Confections.

I cried out at what Tracy had done to my brand-new dog bakery.

CHAPTER TEN

Tracy stood in the café of Confections with her arms outstretched. "You like it?" she asked, beaming.

I unsnapped Sweet Pea's leash and laid her bed in an out-of-the-way cozy corner, where she promptly laid down with a chuff.

Tracy had rearranged the tables and chairs in the café into cozy sitting areas. The feng shui was off the charts. Everything in the display case had been shifted in a good way. My neat was another person's dull, now that Tracy's hands worked their magic. The Peanut Butter Delights laid at angles to each other like dominos instead of my neat pile. The Carrot Bars were lined up like toy soldiers, ramrod straight, and the Ooey Gooey Rich and Chewy Oatmeal Squares were arranged in a pyramid instead of a heap. Sometimes you don't know what you're missing until you see what you'd been missing. For me, it was a display case that made the items enticing.

"How are you so good at this?" I asked.

"Maybe you can get some different lighting," she said politely.

I looked up at the ceiling. It looked fine to me, but I was beginning to question my judgement of what looks fine.

She offered, "Maybe some tiny pin lights and spotlights for the display, and angle the ceiling light fixtures so they're not in the customers' faces while they eat. Well ... while their dogs eat. Hey, can I work for you?"

"What?"

"Please?"

"Do you have any experience working in a dog bakery? Or any bakery?"

"No, but ... I can help with the decorating."

"I need somebody who can help with more than that," I said hesitantly.

She bounced up and down like a kid. "Please? I promise you won't be sorry."

I met her gaze. Thought about it. "Okay, sure. Let's give it a try." I thought I was going to be ordering supplies, baking, cleaning and serving on my own. And that was before I realized how terrible I am at making things look nice. "What about *Pulse*?"

"I'm getting sort of tired getting the short end of the stick there. Nobody even called to tell me about the murder here even though it was my story."

I kneeled down and massaged Sweet Pea's neck.

Tracy said, "I was really beginning to think they didn't want me around and that they hired me just because of my uncle. I mean, I knew he got me in, but I thought once they got to know me, they'd, you know ... like me."

"I'm sure they liked you."

"Could have fooled me. My boss doesn't even pretend to give me good assignments anymore. Ever since she sent me to cover a 'Do Dogs Look Like Their Owners' event and I stayed focused and continued interviewing while a robbery was going on. You'd think she would have appreciated that I completed the job she hired me to do."

I studied her to see if she was kidding. Furrowed brow. Twisted lips. *Nope. Not kidding.*

She said, "I called my boss after you left for the police station and told her I interviewed you and that I would be late getting back to the office because you had to run out." Her eyebrows shot up in indignation. "And she yelled at me!"

I filled Sweet Pea's water bowl and laid it near her bed. "She probably wondered why you weren't going back to work, right?"

"She didn't understand why I was staying here while you were going out, when the whole point of her sending me to you was to find what I could ..." Her mouth closed like a drum.

"Yeah? Find out what you could, huh?" Well, it wasn't like I didn't already know that. *Hello. Journalist. Murder.* I swallowed my disappointment and turned away.

"That's not why I'm here now," she explained. "I was liking talking to you, and being here and meeting Sweet Pea ..."

I nodded. "I understand."

"But you *don't*. I really like being here. It's cheerful and it's full of dog pictures and sweet treats and *you're* so nice …" She implored me with a look I couldn't resist. "Can't I stay?"

Funny thing about desire. Sometimes you want something so much, it lets you make stupid decisions.

"Sure," I said.

But it doesn't mean I'm not going to watch you closely.

CHAPTER ELEVEN

I smoothed back the fur on top of Sweet Pea's head with my hand. Then, I moved on to checking the contents of the small refrigerator up at the display counter.

Tracy continued to fill me in on the things her boss said to her. "She wanted to know how you felt about finding Whitney on your floor and who gave you the rolling pin Whitney was killed with—"

"They didn't say it's how she died. And how does she know about the rolling pin?"

"Everybody knows about the rolling pin. Remember my two co-workers who were here with the camera? They took pictures and video and tweeted a link on Twitter with a full story. Pretty much, everybody in Palm Beach knows it's yours."

Fabulous.

Tracy said, "I told her maybe we should respect the dead and respect you and your new business."

"What did she say?"

"She told me I'm an idiot."

I met her eyes. "Don't let anyone talk to you like that."

She shrugged. "It's a sleazy magazine, anyway."

"Maybe tabloid magazines aren't your calling," I said, trying to add a touch of chipper.

A woman in a pink sweat suit knocked on the locked front door, a black standard poodle at her side. The shocking pink looked striking against the black curls on the dog. "Are you open?" she mouthed through the glass.

Sweet Pea jumped up but stayed back by her bed.

With everything that had happened—finding a dead body on Confections' floor, going to the police station, meeting with the grieving Pamela Goodwin at her house, I had no intention of serving customers that day, though I did stick a batch of Barkin' Cheddar Biscuits into the oven. I ran over to tell Pinky we'd open the following day rather than force her to read my lips. I unlocked the door but kept myself between the opening so neither her dog nor mine—*Mine! I have a dog!*—could muzzle their way in or out. "We won't be open until tomorrow," I said. "But do you mind if I pet your dog?"

"Sure. This is Patsy."

Sweet Pea started to make her way over. "Hold on, girl." One dog on a leash, the other not. Not a good plan for a happy dynamic.

The owner said, "She likes other dogs."

"Even if they're off a leash?"

Hesitantly, she said, "I think so."

"How about we don't take any chances?" I had enough grief for one day. Then, to Tracy, "Would you mind moving Sweet Pea's bed to the back for now?"

I needed to work some things out. I couldn't banish Sweet Pea to the back every time a dog came in. "I'm afraid we're not technically open yet, but Patsy is welcome to a treat on the house."

"Come on, Sweet Pea, let's go to the back," Tracy said.

Sweet Pea peered over at me.

"It's okay, girl," I said and marveled at how quickly we connected.

Tracy led the way to the back.

I opened the door for the woman and Patsy, who immediately headed to the display case. I could have sworn the woman was sneaking glances at the floor where Whitney had been lying.

Tracy returned.

"How about a Peanut Butter Delight for Patsy and an espresso for you?" I asked. "Free of charge."

"I smell cheddar cheese." She eyed the items in the case. "Do you have anything for people?"

"Sorry. Just the espresso."

Tracy and I gathered the items and handed them to our two guests, who then sat at a café table.

The sneaky-petes out on the sidewalk saw the action and flooded into Canine Confections. *So much for waiting until tomorrow to let customers in.* I began to set up espresso cups and napkins to give away as freebies, but when a customer without a dog asked where Whitney's body had been lying, I changed my plan.

I guided everybody out. "Please come back tomorrow when we have our grand opening!" Staying open would do more harm than good.

Tracy helped me shuffle everyone to the front door.

"Bye, Patsy," I called out to the poodle.

My cell rang as I locked the front door and leaned against it. I pulled the custom-made blinds down for privacy and answered.

"Hate to bother you again so soon," Detective Trumble said. "Everything okay over there?"

"Sure. Why?" I moved to the back room for privacy, sat at my desk and rubbed Sweet Pea's butt.

"Just making sure," Trumble said. "I asked my local guy over your way to keep an eye on things and he said a woman complained that you shoved them out of your dog bakery."

"We didn't shove anybody. Do you think someone is trying to start trouble for me?"

The silence at the other end of the phone spoke volumes.

The hair on the back of my neck stood up. "*Do* you think somebody is trying to get rid of me and Canine Confections?" I whispered into the phone as though Sweet Pea might overhear and get upset. "And frame me for Whitney's death? I mean, she was murdered, right?"

This was met with more silence.

I could hear my voice shake. "Tell me I'm being paranoid."

After a few moments, Trumble said from his end of the phone, "Sorry, Miss Armstrong. I can't give you any information."

CHAPTER TWELVE

I hung up with Trumble and rubbed my arms up and down like when I'm chilly, even though the oven was on. Whether or not the detective had an idea of who the murderer was didn't matter. He obviously didn't have enough evidence to bring them in, *whoever* it was.

I called Whitney's house since I had forgotten to ask Robert for the name of the shelter, then called the shelter. "Hi, my name is Samantha Armstrong. How would I go about adopting a dog you adopted to Whitney Goodwin a couple of weeks ago?"

"What? Adopting a dog—"

"A woman named Whitney Goodwin adopted a Lab Mix recently," I said.

"Do you know how many dogs we have?"

"Her name is Sweet Pea."

Sweet Pea's ears twitched. I reached down and rubbed them.

"What date was she adopted?"

"I don't know," I said.

"Hold on a second." The swoosh of the broom in the café sounded through the door. A riffle of papers from the other end of the phone, and the woman said, "I found it. Whitney Goodwin. She has to come in and sign if she's letting you take the dog."

"She can't do that."

"Why not?"

You mean there's one person in Palm Beach who doesn't know Whitney was murdered?

"She …" I started.

"You could just keep her, except if you don't get the dog signed over, she can take her back anytime."

My next call would be to Whitney's parents. Before I hung up with the shelter, I said, "While I have you … were you the one who adopted Sweet Pea out to Whitney?"

"No. That was … wait a minute. That was Danny."

"Can I speak with him please?"

"He's not here. He'll be in tomorrow morning."

I didn't know what I expected Danny to tell me, but any morsel would do … if Whitney was with anyone when she came in, if she seemed happy, if she was on her cell arguing with anybody …

I thanked the shelter employee, called the Goodwins, and asked Robert if he would get the paperwork to the Goodwins to sign Sweet Pea over to me. He said that he would. I thanked him and hung up, then stared at the wall behind my desk. "If Trumble would hurry up and find the killer, I wouldn't have to worry about getting answers myself," I said out loud, completely ignoring the fact that Whitney had been killed only that day.

"What do you mean?" Tracy asked, her pixie face peeking in the door separating the front of Confections from the back.

"What are you doing back here?" I snapped. "Sorry. I didn't mean that." And I didn't. I just didn't particularly feel comfortable with her sneaking up on me or listening to me talk to myself. Chances were good she was doing neither, and I was simply on edge. I inhaled deeply and said, "Of course you're welcome to come back here. You just took me by surprise."

"Are you sure?" Tracy asked. "Because my boss ... I mean my ex-boss at *Pulse* made me knock."

"Of course. You need to get back here. And what do you mean your ex-boss? You quit?" I thought she would at least keep it as a side gig.

"Yup," she said with a wide grin. "I just called her. What were you saying about Trumble?"

"I just wish he would find out who murdered Whitney."

"He will. He's known for being as stubborn as a dog with a bone." She turned to Sweet Pea. "No offense."

The three of us made our way out front. Sweet Pea sniffed the tables, the display case, and the front door, I suspect, to gather intel about who had been in her space. I wondered what kind of message Patsy the poodle left.

"But he's treating me like I'm a suspect," I complained.

"Guilty until proven innocent," Tracy said with a shrug. "Trumble takes pride in keeping the town 'clean of crime,' as he likes to say. He's almost due to retire and thinks this is his last shot at making a name for himself."

"He has to know I didn't kill Whitney."

"Why does he have to know that?" she asked innocently.

I found myself explaining to her, "Because I would never do that! Why would I *do* that?"

"I don't know. Why would *anyone?*" She polished the display case until it shone, looking up at me as she wiped. Something stirred behind her eyes. I was *sure* she was no dummy. I'd have to wait to find out. Meanwhile, so far, she had only been a help to me.

"Whitney's bakery is for people, mine is for dogs. So assuming I am not the kind of person who is capable of murdering my competition, I have no motive for killing Whitney."

Tracy seemed to consider that for a second, nodded her head one time and went back to checking the gloss on the case.

I grabbed Sweet Pea's leash. "Sweet Pea, want to give me an excuse to meet the people in the neighborhood?"

She returned my question with a wag of her tail.

Tracy finished wiping the display case and began placing the gold-lined napkins in a criss-cross design one on top of another.

"We're closed, so I guess you can leave. Just give me the keys from the locksmith."

"I almost forgot!" she said with a laugh and handed them to me. I looked at the two sets of keys in the palm of my hand, hesitating about giving her a set so soon in our relationship. I chewed the inside of my mouth, decided to procrastinate my decision, and set the extra set on the desk in back.

"Do you mind if I stay?" she asked. "I'm not done with the napkins."

I studied her. *What's your story?*

My eyes scanned the café, display, marveled at her handiwork with the treats. "Don't let anyone in."

"Ay, ay, commander!" she said and saluted me, hand to forehead before bending over and focusing with eyes like lasers on the napkins. I could almost see the wheels turning, figuring out the best angle for each one.

Out on the sidewalk, my head swam, and not from the humidity. I'd never been involved in a criminal case of any kind, let alone a murder in my own dog bakery. I'd find the answers one fact at a time. Eventually—I hoped—they'd add up. I'm big on hope.

Bethany would be a fine first neighbor to get to know. Well, second, after Martha. *Oh, third!* How could I forget Sexy Stubble?

I gently knocked on the glass door of Gallery Bebe and waited for Bethany to saunter up from the back. When she arrived, she stepped outside her door and smoothed her sleek ponytail back with manicured fingers. Pale green. Her features were as sharp as any business owner I've known. Which, granted, isn't a long list, but the short list contained a couple of friends of Aunt Mary's whom I knew to be millionaires. I suspected the artists whose works Bethany commissioned for her gallery paid dearly for the privilege.

"Bethany Westwood? I'm your new neighbor, Samantha Armstrong."

Sweet Pea tried cozying up to her, but Bethany shook her leg, presumably, to keep the fluffball at bay.

"I'm sorry. Are you afraid of dogs?" I asked.

"No."

"I forget sometimes that not everyone likes them."

"I like them fine," she said. She paused and stared at Sweet Pea, then back at me. "Is there something I can help you with?"

"I just wanted to introduce myself and get to know my neighbors."

She stared at me, silent and expressionless. Bethany had the fresh complexion of someone who stepped out of a steam and facial twenty minutes ago. Between that and her shiny hair, she gave the appearance of someone I had seen before. Suddenly it came to me: She was a combination of models from magazine covers. Glamorous yet seemingly a natural beauty.

"Geez, you're really pretty," I said.

Bethany gave me a polite smile but said nothing.

When I couldn't take the silence any longer, I said, "I assume you know what happened this morning."

She tilted her head at me. "What do you think?"

Well, aren't *you* a slice of sweet apple pie?

In the polite tone I saved for such occasions, I said, "I wonder if maybe you could tell me if you saw anything ... strange?"

"I already answered questions from the police."

I took a breath and began again. "But you know how the mind sometimes takes a while to catch up to what's happened? I thought maybe that happened to you. You know, that you thought of something since speaking with them."

"That doesn't happen to me." She crossed her arms in front of her and gazed at me like I was a science project.

"Today was supposed to be my grand opening, and I want to get a handle on things so I know how to proceed."

She unfolded her arms and let them drop to her sides. "You're asking me when you should have your grand opening? What did the police say? Do they know who killed Whitney?" She paused. "Do *you*?" The smallest of smiles crept on to her lips.

"No. I don't. How about you?" I said and smiled sweetly. Two can play *this* game.

I think I burst her bubble because her balloon deflated maybe a quarter of an inch, not unlike Whitney's when I didn't let her kowtow me about the rumors. I could see Bethany and I becoming either enemies or good friends. She said, "I have no idea who killed her." Then, "People seem very interested in your bakery." The small smile could have been pleasant or smirky. I decided to start fresh and take it as the former.

"Yeah. It hasn't been the best start. And it's a *dog* bakery," I mumbled.

Bethany relaxed her rigid posture. "That's what Whitney said."

"She talked about it? Well, see, there's something interesting!"

The scathing look she gave me told me she disagreed. "What is so interesting about Whitney telling me you were opening a dog bakery?"

"Plenty! How did she feel about it? Was she glad that we would have a little strip of Worth Avenue for shoppers to take a break?" I tried to see if Whitney herself was the one who was unhappy about Confections. "She didn't mind a dog bakery two doors away, did she?"

Bethany's eyes met mine but only for a moment. "I don't know how she felt about it. It's not like we were best friends."

"Did you talk to anyone else about Confections?"

"See, now that amazes me."

"What does?" I asked, finally happy the ice was thawing.

"How you could completely turn the murder of one of our local residents into something about *you*."

"What? No, I—"

"I know, I know. Whitney was found on your floor. But unless you killed her, it really has nothing to do with you, does it?"

I flashed my eyes at the dewy witch. "Well, I *hope* not ..."

"Or does it?" she asked.

I sighed, said, "See you later," and started to leave with Sweet Pea.

"I suppose something that's interesting is Rick was roaming around earlier than usual this morning," Bethany called after me.

I almost turned around and responded with "Sexy Stubble?" but caught myself. Instead, I asked, "From Sophisticated Pet?"

92 | Paws for Concern

"He probably heard about the new dog bakery opening up two doors from his store and wanted to see the competition."

"I'm not his competition. He sells pet supplies."

Bethany shrugged. "You know how competitive some people can get."

I pretended that thought hadn't crossed my mind. "That still doesn't explain why he'd kill Whitney."

"I didn't say he killed Whitney."

"You just—"

"I said he was roaming around earlier than usual this morning and he was maybe interested to see the competition for himself."

"But I'm *not* his competition!" I took a deep breath. We were going in circles.

Sweet Pea shifted on her paws and licked my hand.

"Oh well," Bethany said. "Tomorrow's another day."

Finally. A drop of sunshine.

She smoothed her hair back. "Then again, it can't be a good sign when you find a dead body on your floor first thing in the morning."

CHAPTER THIRTEEN

For the briefest of moments, I wanted to drive back to Whitehall Estate and snuggle in my cottage with a fleece blanket, mug of hot cocoa—never mind I live in South Florida—and Sweet Pea, instead of deal with my new life. Bethany had really gotten to me.

But only for a second. On the short walk from Gallery Bebe to Canine Confections, I made up my mind that, as I told the customers a few minutes earlier, the next day would be my grand opening. No more waiting around for the right time or for the police to tell me I had the all-clear. Or for an art gallery owner to give me the okay. *When exactly had I become so meek?*

I threw open the front door, surprising Tracy, who was maneuvering the pictures on the walls.

"You don't mind, do you?" she asked.

Her eye for placement increased the visual appeal of Canine Confections exponentially. I was looking for cozy and elegant. Tracy was able to create it. "Looks great."

"Then why the sour puss?"

I unsnapped Sweet Pea's leash. She gave Tracy a quick lick before sniffing the empty spot on the floor where Whitney was lying that morning.

"I'm getting the sneaking suspicion that Detective Trumble is right. The residents aren't too happy about me."

Tracy bobbed her head up and down. "Yup. 'Killing one of our own.'"

"What?"

"I mean, not killing. You know. I'm just saying what *they're* saying."

"Who? *Who* is saying that?"

Tracy stepped back and considered a large photo with a golden retriever licking an ice cream cone. Absently, she said, "You know. Everybody."

"Everybody is saying I killed Whitney?"

Tracy shrugged. "Not in those words exactly."

I tried again. "Is there anyone in particular who's throwing me under the bus?"

"No," she said with a cheerful smile. "Don't worry, no one in particular has it in for you. It's the general consensus."

"It's the general consensus?" I didn't mean to keep repeating what she said but I kept repeating what she said because, *oh my God they all think I'm a murderer.*

"Are you alright?" she asked. "I don't think I ever saw anyone's face turn that color before." Tracy hurried over to my side.

"I'm fine." But Whitney and her parents deserved answers. Also, I didn't want Canine Confections' reputation as a murder site to solidify, especially since Aunt Mary was bankrolling it. Something happens, gets resolved, people forget and move on to the next thing. But when something happens and remains in the air—unresolved crime like a murder, for instance—people tend to hang on until it becomes the new norm. The last thing I wanted was for my dog bakery to follow in the footsteps of houses that are turned into a Murder House on bus tours. I could hear the overhead speakers on the West Palm Diva Duck Tour now: "Canine Confections, a must-see Murder Site on Worth Avenue."

I would see what I could get out of Aunt Mary that night and call Danny at the shelter the next morning. I shut my worries up for the moment and focused on the next morning's opening. I was sure the mayor wouldn't have another open slot in his day for me, so I would have to make a splash without him. I got started by showing Tracy where I kept the baking supplies, ingredients and baking schedule, and moved on to the ins-and-outs of the dog bakery business. Tracy needed to know more about working here than how to arrange pictures and organize the dog treats. In the back room, I waved my arm at the shelves and refrigerator. "I buy organic and use only high-quality ingredients. They're worth the cost and the people here can afford it."

"Can I help you make the Pawty Cookies I saw in your brochure on the counter?"

"I'm counting on it," I said.

We spent the rest of the afternoon preparing for my second grand opening, slated for the following morning. I decided to make a fresh batch of Carrot Squares even though we had plenty of goodies. Sweet Pea, a Labrador-Mix who was very unparticular about what she put in her mouth, made herself available should any morsel of *yum* drop to the floor.

By the time Tracy and I had finished in the evening, we were both covered in flour and brain-clogged from the information dump. We said good-bye with tired smiles, and Sweet Pea and I scampered over to Sophisticated Pet. Rick wasn't there, but in his place was a pretty saleswoman. I loosened the lead on Sweet Pea's leash and let her pad around for a minute to let me know what she found most interesting. Since dog treats were high on her list of what she found interesting, and she had plenty of those from Confections, I picked out a squeaky toy and a bag of three tennis balls. I scanned the store as the saleswoman rang up the toy. Nothing out of the ordinary. No men in dark raincoats holding a rolling pin hiding in the aisles.

"I bet it's fun working here," I said to the woman.

"It is. The best part is the dogs."

"And the owner?"

"Rick?" She laughed and squeaked the toy. "If I weren't happily married, I would be running up and down these aisles after him.

Sweet Pea, excited by the squeak, began dancing on the pads of her paws.

As we exited the store, I noticed a jar with dog treats. He had mentioned having a few snacks here, but I didn't know he had them right at the door.

Back at the car, I opened the passenger side for Sweet Pea, tossed the toys inside, climbed into the driver's seat, and headed for home, breathing in the salt air from the ocean to our right. I kept a steady speed on Ocean Boulevard, hardly able to believe I lived here in Palm Beach after hearing so much about it growing up. The town is as much a state of mind as an actual island in South Florida. Between the royal palm trees, the ocean, and the residents driving to their estates in their E-Class Mercedes (they save the Rolls and Lamborghinis for special occasions), you almost feel like you've left the drab old world for someplace shiny and new ... except Palm Beach *isn't* new. Its architecture harkens to the good-old days, when a famous architect named Addison Mizner made merry with his designs. The buildings, whether huge estates, condo apartments or houses, frequently have an opulence from the town's pre-Depression glory days, when Mizner was designing palaces all over Palm Beach. Everywhere, you see terra-cotta roofs and arched windows, courtyards and balconies. That is, if the gates to the property happen to be open or the hedge is unusually low.

I turned on the car radio and heard the tail end of a report announcing that the police had determined Whitney's was a "wrongful death." My stomach felt like it fell to the plush suede of my driver's seat. Anxiously, I kept my eyes on the road in front of me. I came upon the one estate whose low hedges and clean lines stood in stark contrast to the high hedges and crenellated roofs that surrounded it, then on to my aunt's. Pulling up to her electronic gate, I pressed the code, waited a moment for the gates to open, then slowly drove down her long driveway, checking the windows of the Big House as I passed as if she would be waving her arms at one of them if she were in distress. We pulled up to our cottage, and oh, how I loved my corner of the world. Bright red hibiscus blossoms crawled across the trellis, a stone walkway led up to the front door, and palm tree fronds swayed in front of my kitchen window.

I opened the front door, unclipped Sweet Pea's leash and announced, "Welcome to your new home."

She wagged her tail tentatively and began sniffing, first the front entrance, then the kitchen, living room, then the back bedrooms and bath. I positioned her placemat and water bowl in a corner of the kitchen and showed her where it was, then changed into my bathing suit while she continued to investigate her new home. Next, we trekked over to the Big House to check on Aunt Mary. Soon as I opened the front door, the hollowness of the large, empty foyer greeted us. I wasn't sure if Aunt Mary was still napping, but I needed to make sure she was okay. I tiptoed further inside, but after only a moment of hesitation, Sweet Pea began to run around the hardwood floors of the foyer. She slipped, slid into a wall, wagged her tail with glee, and did it again. The *tap, tap tap* of her toenails on the floors echoed off the walls and high ceiling. It only then dawned on me that I had never asked Aunt Mary if it was okay for Sweet Pea to live with us. What had I been thinking? A little voice in my head answered: *Maybe about murder?*

If my aunt said it wasn't okay, I didn't know what I'd do, but bringing Sweet Pea back to the shelter wasn't an option. I Scarlett O'Hara'd that worry for another day.

I moseyed into the kitchen with Sweet Pea at my heels, in search of Aunt Mary. I then marveled—like I always do—at the backyard through the windows. One of my favorite things about the house was the huge kitchen with windows that looked out on acres of lush landscape and fruit trees—orange, lemon, lime, even a cocktail tree. With no aunt in sight, we wandered into her bedroom, where she was lying on her bed quietly snoring.

We made our way back out the long hallway and out the front door, then out the gate and down to the beach. Since I had moved to Palm Beach, I tried to swim at least five times a week. Now that I had Sweet Pea, I thought she might like to chase the waves. Swimming in the evening is uplifting and relaxing to the extreme. It also makes cocktail hour and dinner that much more fulfilling. Unlike some of the other houses on Ocean Drive, Aunt Mary didn't have her own tunnel to the beach. But as luck would have it, a little entrance existed right down the block. Few knew of it, so it was my own little piece of Palm Beach pie.

I hadn't been sure how Sweet Pea would feel about the beach, but she loved it. She ran and chased seagulls until I waded through the crash of the waves and into the water. Then, too scared to brave the waves herself, and too loyal—even to *me* whom had she just met—to leave me in those scary-looking waters, she looked at me with concern the entire time I swam. *So* much concern that I thought maybe next time I'd leave her at home so she could relax and enjoy some downtime off watch-duty. As I completed my last few strokes, I called out, "I'm fine!"

Her ears perked up and she paced back and forth on the wet sand where the water cascaded over her little white feet. While I trudged through the crash of the waves back to shore, I thought about Whitney and how she would never again be able to enjoy the simple pleasure of an ocean swim. The concern Sweet Pea showed me made me wonder how Whitney's parents showed *theirs* for their daughter. I decided I would broach the subject with Aunt Mary at cocktail hour.

Sweet Pea ran over to me as soon as I got through the crash of the waves. She wagged her tail and ran up and down the shoreline as I wrapped a turquoise and shocking pink beach towel around myself.

"Come on, wiggly worm, I have to get this leash on you." She settled down enough that I could click it on, and we slogged up the sand to Ocean Boulevard.

Feeling relaxed, refreshed, and anxious to ask Aunt Mary what she knew about Whitney's parents, Sweet Pea and I buzzed ourselves into Whitehall and returned to the cottage, where I changed into dry clothes. Then we darted over to the Big House, where I hoped we would find Aunt Mary up and feeling like her snazzy self and not at all perturbed that I'd brought a dog home.

She was sitting in the cozy kitchen nook looking out the side window that led to the pool and tennis court. Sweet Pea ran up and licked her arm.

"Be careful of Aunt Mary's knee, sweet girl."

"Look who's here!" my aunt said delightedly and rubbed Sweet Pea's head.

"Whitney's mother was going to return her to the shelter."

"Well, we can't have that. She'll move in with us."

"You don't mind?"

"Of course not. I suppose you want her to stay with you in the cottage, but she can come over to the house anytime. It'll be nice to have some life in here."

The thrice-weekly staff and chef was hardly company for my aunt. Alice was a help when Aunt Mary needed her to pick up the *New York Times* or shop for a gift for a friend's birthday, but it meant she didn't need to be at the house.

"There are plenty of other dogs who need homes at the shelter, if you're looking for company." I laughed lightly. "Maybe we'll wait until your knee heals before we have you running around these hallways after a four-legged little one."

I helped Aunt Mary up from the table as I had been doing every evening at that time. She didn't like needing the help and was stubborn about trying to move around on her own.

"Do you think it would be a good idea to hire a nurse until you heal up?" I asked. "Not that I mind, but I'm not going to be here that much during the days."

"I don't need anyone full time. I just like to have family around," she said and pinched my cheek. She shook her head. "I still can't believe your parents were willing to miss your grand opening."

Holding her slow and steady as we walked through the foyer, I said, "We've been through this. My father bought the cruise tickets a year ago, before I had any idea I would be opening a dog bakery."

She shuffled alongside of me. "And he didn't get the cancellation insurance. My baby brother, Mr. Cheapskate," she said with the soft smile brothers and sisters reserve for their much-maligned but much-beloved siblings.

"I could have waited to open so they could be here."

Aunt Mary snickered.

"What?" I asked.

"It's just the thought of you waiting struck me as ..." She held a hand to her mouth.

"Okay. I know. I can get a little impatient sometimes."

Luckily for Aunt Mary, Whitehall was a mansion with an elevator, among other luxuries, so we didn't have to worry about climbing up and down long staircases. We made our way to it for cocktail hour. Or cocktail *half*-hour. In Palm Beach, the upper-class have their ceremonies, and the cocktail hour is one of their favorites. Aunt Mary might have only married into this lifestyle, but she'd been living with it for so many years that she continued the rituals after my uncle died. Cocktail hour with Aunt Mary doesn't necessarily mean alcoholic beverages. Mostly, she says, because it would ruin the rest of her evening by making her want to do nothing but sleep. But she—and now I—enjoyed creating our own versions of cocktails for the fun of it. Perrier with a splash of lemon from the lemon and lime cocktail tree in her yard. Fresh carrot juice with a slice of beet. Iced tea with plenty of ice and a large lime wedge, again, from the cocktail trees. Once my aunt was more mobile, I wanted to invite her to the cottage for cocktail hour sometimes. There were so *many* things I wanted to do ...

"What are we having tonight?" she asked.

"You have to wait," I teased.

She smiled and leaned on her cane as we entered the elevator. I held myself back from gripping her arm.

My friends back in Sun Haven were probably not attending cocktail hour. Most would be either at the gym after work, or meeting friends, or helping their parents prepare dinner since many of them still lived at home. But I'd come to look forward to the ritual. Not only because it had helped me and my aunt grow closer, but also because it gave me a sense of sameness, stability, something to count on. If I worked in an office, I would have my co-workers, desk, coffee machine. My old boss Debbie used to meet me for a cup of coffee in the morning before heading to Debbie's Bakery. I worked for myself now, and I was living in a new town, far from everything that was familiar except for my aunt.

As the three of us rode up in the elevator, Sweet Pea looked about nervously at the shaking box. The doors opened and she zoomed out to the second floor, then roamed around the sitting room while Aunt Mary made herself comfortable on the velvet couch and I prepared a mini-pitcher of Pellegrino with a squeeze of lime. We sat up here because Aunt Mary liked the idea of sitting in a cozy spot. Aside from the nook in the kitchen, finding a cozy spot in a mansion was no minor feat. I'd wondered if Aunt Mary enjoyed all this space. When I had asked her, her eyes misted as she detailed all her memories in each room with my Uncle Joseph. New Year's Eves in the ballroom, late-night suppers in the kitchen after a night attending an opera at the Kravis Center … she wouldn't move any time soon. Maybe half-past never.

Not wanting to leave the girl out, I served her fresh cold water and frozen green beans since she'd had several treats from Canine Confections already that day. She sniffed at the bean, gave me a dirty look, I'm sure of it … and walked away.

Sometimes during cocktail hour, we called my parents, but since they were off gallivanting on a cruise, it gave me a great excuse to spend the time asking Aunt Mary about Whitney and her parents.

Tact was not one of those things that came naturally to me. I sipped and stared at the plush carpet, not knowing how to approach the subject of asking her about people she knew without sounding like I was blaming them for anything, least of all their daughter's death.

"What's on your mind?" she asked from her perch on the couch.

"I talked to Bethany today." *Wimp,* I said to myself for avoiding the topic of Whitney's parents. "Do you know her? She runs Gallery Bebe?"

Aunt Mary sipped. "I've shopped on Worth Avenue enough times. Pretty girl."

"Very. I hear she's from around here?"

"What about her, honey?"

"Was she friends with Whitney?"

My aunt settled back on the couch. "They're about the same age, aren't they? *Your* age, as a matter of fact."

The furry girl roamed around the cozy sitting area, turned in a wolfy, "I'm making a bed in the woods" circle, and settled onto the carpet, where her eyes began to close.

"She looks a little sleepy," I said. "It was a big day for her."

"For you too," my aunt said.

I got comfy in my chair and set my Pellegrino down on the coffee table. "How is your knee?"

"It's fine. What are you not wanting to talk to me about?"

Clever, clever Auntie Mary. "It's nothing I can't handle."

"Oh, I'm sure of that. It doesn't mean you have to keep it all inside you. It's not good for the digestion."

I laughed and cuddled a velvet pillow into my chest. "Sweet Pea was watching me in the waves, and it made me think about love and loyalty and the lengths people would go for someone they love."

Her eyes shimmered at me.

"Have I thanked you enough for believing in me and my dog bakery?" I asked.

"Let me see," she teased. "I think you only thanked me five times today."

"Can you tell me anything about Whitney's parents?"

She nodded, like this was the answer to her question of what was on my mind. "Nice couple. Spoiled their daughter, like anyone would."

"Spoiled how?"

"The usual. A good education. Cars, vacations, clothes."

I distractedly sipped my cocktail while I imagined the length a parent would go for a child. "Anything else? More … unique?"

Aunt Mary frowned at me. "What do you mean by unique?"

I swung my legs up and curled my sock-feet under me to make myself small as if to focus on the one pinpoint of our girl Whitney Goodwin. "Did they do anything out of the ordinary for her?"

My aunt shook her head. "I don't think so."

Hmmmm. Well, this wasn't going well.

"Tracy said they pulled strings," I said. "Gave her money."

Aunt Mary gently laughed. "That's not unique around here."

"No. I suppose not."

"Giving money and getting friends to do favors is just another day." Her eyelids slipped shut and snapped open.

A bell rang in my head. "What kind of favors?"

She waved her hand. "Oh. I don't know. Whatever they need."

I didn't mean to grill her, but I wanted to know. "Do you think they might have done something besides give her money to open Patisserie?"

"Now that you mention it, I heard something about a roster."

"What kind of roster?"

"You know. A list." She put her finger to her chin. "Or was it a register? Maybe I'm thinking of a cash register … the money they gave her for her pastry shop. Oh, my mind is a muddle with this ridiculous painkiller in me. I'm going to throw the bottle out right now." She started to get up from her chair until I ran over and sat her back down.

"Will you please be careful?" I asked firmly. "Or do you want me to call your surgeon and see how *he* feels about you up and around only a month after knee surgery?"

"It was orthoscopic. A tiny little procedure."

"I'm pretty sure he doesn't want you popping up and down so much."

Aunt Mary waved me away like a pesky mosquito. "You, Samantha Armstrong, are a nag."

I gave a firm nod. "And will continue to be until you're back at one-hundred percent. So tell me more about this roster or register or whatever."

She pooh-poohed that. "Don't listen to me." She grimaced in pain even though her eyes were shutting. "I wouldn't want to add to the rest of them and make things even more murky."

"The rest of who?"

"People who like to talk."

Funny, that was exactly what I was looking for. "Actually, I'm pretty interested to hear what they have to say."

"Not all of them. Haven't you ever known people who like to stir things up?"

I shrugged and nodded.

"Watch out for bald-face liars," my aunt said.

"Aunt Mary! This doesn't sound like you."

She tried to stretch her leg out but didn't quite make it. "I'm afraid I might be getting a little cranky from the pain. Would you get me some ice, please?"

I jumped up and ran over to the mini frig and freezer, then placed the ice gently on top of her knee.

The tension in her face relaxed as she leaned back against the couch. "Mmmm, thank you." She peeked over at me. "What else is on your mind? I could always tell by your leg bobbing up and down that there's something going on in that pretty little head of yours."

I took a swig from my glass. "Alright, aside from feeling awful for Whitney and her parents, I'm afraid what it will do to our business."

"*Your* business."

"Okay, my business. With your money. Ever since I found her on Canine Confections' floor this morning, the more I talk to people, the more it seems like they're blaming me."

"It hasn't even been a day. And I'm not sure people are blaming you because they think you are to blame. It sets their mind at ease that they can put their finger on who did this. Once they find who it is, they'll forget all about blaming you. You'll see."

"I'm not so sure. You know how once a restaurant gets a bad name, it's hard to build trust in them again? Tracy said everyone is pretty much thinking I'm cursed or something, like I carted a dead body into town. She said they might boycott."

Aunt Mary got quiet.

"What are you thinking?" I asked.

She shook her head slightly and shrugged. "Nothing much."

"Go ahead and say it, whatever it is," I said.

My aunt hesitated a moment. "Are you certain she doesn't have any ulterior motives?"

"It's not like I haven't thought that myself but … I'm pretty sure she's sincere and wants to help me."

Aunt Mary chuckled.

Exasperated, I said, "What now?"

"I would think that after Peter and your friend, you might not be so trusting."

Yeah. No kidding. "Just because my boyfriend and best friend got together and broke my heart in two places doesn't mean I'll let that change who I am."

She reached over and patted my cheek. "Good for you."

I sipped my cocktail and felt the cool liquid refresh my throat. "On to another subject, Bethany said that Rick from the pet store was hanging around earlier this morning, so I guess I'll keep an eye on him."

I wanted to see if Aunt Mary knew anything more, but she rested her head back against the couch again.

"Are you alright?"

"Will you stop asking me that, please?"

I forced my mouth shut and we spent the rest of cocktail hour in pleasant conversation. Afterward, we rode down the elevator to dine on Chef Luca's from-scratch vegetable stew and crusty French bread in the warm and comfy kitchen nook. I piled the stew into Aunt Mary's porcelain bowl and cracked about a quarter cup of fresh pepper on top per her request. As I twisted the pepper mill side to side, an image of the sickening angle of Whitney's head made me gag.

I coughed.

"Are you okay, sweetheart?" Aunt Mary asked.

Clearing my throat, I said, "I forgot Sweet Pea's food in the cottage."

"Can she eat something else for tonight so you don't have to run over there?"

"Mind if I snag a couple of eggs and a hunk of cheese? I'll make her an omelet."

"Sounds delicious."

My aunt dug into her stew while I prepared Sweet Pea's omelet. I guess it tasted okay because she ate it in three bites.

"Tomorrow morning should be fun," Aunt Mary said from over her bowl of stew.

I sat down to my own dinner. "It *should* be, yes. *Today* should have been fun too."

"You can't let that get you down."

I chuckled. "You sound like my mother. Miss Sally Sunshine."

"My brother married a smart woman."

We spent the next few minutes mostly in silence as we finished our meal. I jumped up from the table when I remembered the chilled raspberries and carton of whipped cream in the refrigerator. I whipped the cream up in a jiffy and laid the two bowls of berries on the table.

"Zero calories," I lied.

"How do you get it so nice and creamy? Do you add something to stiffen it?"

"Nope," I said and scooped a spoonful of cream on top of each bowl of berries. "That's only if I need it to last for a while. I use cornstarch or powdered sugar. This is just cream, au natural!"

I dolloped a small bit of cream into Sweet Pea's dish. She lapped it up.

"That's okay for her?" my aunt asked.

"In small doses. Coffee tonight?"

"Decaf?" she asked.

"Of course." Three o'clock in the morning comes fast when you go to bed much past nine. But the decaf I bought was a delicious, rich roast I'd found at a farmer's market in West Palm Beach, the town about twenty royal palm trees away from *the* Palm Beach.

As we sipped, I tip-toed to the subject I'd been dying to ask. "Am I allowed to ask about you and the detective now?"

She waved her hand in a dismissive gesture. "There's not much to tell."

"Are you two ..." I didn't know what term to use. "Seeing each other?"

Aunt Mary laughed and pulled out her puzzle roll-up mat. "Is that what they're calling it these days?"

I shrugged and looked for a sharp pencil in the cup on the counter by the phone.

She unrolled the mat. "Well, if you must know…"

"Yes. I must," I said and laughed.

"One night, after we finally figured out that I'd been putting the wrong code into the security system, I asked him if he'd like a slice of pie. Ever since, one of us calls the other from time to time, and we visit and try different flavors of pie. You know I like to bake."

"And that's it?"

"For now, at least. Who knows if it will turn into something more? Meanwhile, I'm sure he'll be a little more open with this Whitney case than he normally would be."

"Really? That strikes me as strange. He seems like such a professional."

The redness that colored her face told me everything I needed to know.

I eased off. Why push? From the sounds of it, I'd be more in the loop on the case than the average dog bakery owner who walked in on a dead body.

Over coffee, Aunt Mary fit pieces of her Thomas Kinkaid puzzle together and I worked on a crossword puzzle. There's nothing like fitting a letter into a neat little box to let you know all is right with the world.

A few minutes into my crossword, I pulled out a notepad from the basket Aunt Mary keeps on the kitchen counter. "I'm writing a list of things I need to get from the grocery store. Do you need anything?"

She grinned as she snapped a puzzle piece in place. "Alice can do that for you."

"It's okay. I like to grocery shop."

"What do you need?" Generous to a fault, Aunt Mary gestured to her refrigerator and cabinets.

"Nothing from you!" I said and laughed.

A funny look crossed her face.

"What?" I asked.

"Something about what we were talking about earlier …"

I wrote down *food for Sweet Pea* on my list while she thought about it.

"A list!" she cried. "That's it. Whitney's parents got her on some kind of list."

"For Patisserie?"

"Yes. Well, I assume so. Like I said, I probably shouldn't say anything. I don't want to add to everybody else's gossip."

Tracy *said* her parents pulled strings. I thought it was just about the money.

When Aunt Mary had no other information to give me, we spent the rest of our time together enjoying our puzzles and light conversation. After an hour, Aunt Mary went off to watch TV and Sweet Pea and I made our way back to the cottage. She ran inside and waited for me to settle someplace. I chose the couch, snuggled with a blanket and my precious peanut, and called Tracy.

"I thought we pretty much covered everything today," Tracy said lightly after she picked up. "Think of something else?"

"Always!" I said with a laugh. "What do you think of handing out free samples of the Creamy Cheese Drops outside the front door tomorrow to attract attention?"

"Like we did today?"

"Most of the people today were only there to see the crime scene. I want to attract the attention of our customers. The dog owners." I ran my hand down Sweet Pea's back in long, even strokes.

"That'd be good."

"Excellent. So …" I tried for casual. "I was thinking it might be fun to start doing some marketing with the other pet-type stores in the area. What do you think?"

She had to have wondered why I was calling her with this non-urgent message when we'd be seeing each other in another eight hours. But if she did, she didn't say. "I'll have to think about all the other stores that sell pet stuff."

I already did that but yes, keep going …

"The only store I can think of is Rick's."

Bingo.

She said, "I'm sure he'll be happy for you guys to put your heads together on this."

"Yeah? Okay, great." I rubbed Sweet Pea's front paw with my index finger. She laid all the way back, lifted her hind leg, and showed me her tummy to rub. "So, he's a nice guy, then?"

"Rick? Oh yeah. He's owned Sophisticated Pet for years. It's everybody's favorite place to go with their dogs."

The reporter in her didn't catch on that I was digging for info. I didn't know her that well yet, but if her hand was still in the cookie jar at *Pulse*, I needed to be careful. There was a very good chance Rick wasn't threatened by my dog bakery and hadn't thrown a dead body in it to thwart its success. If that was the case, I didn't want Tracy writing an article bashing the poor guy.

"It's everybody's favorite place to bring their dogs, huh?" I asked.

"Yeah. Well, you know. It's the only place on Worth. Except yours now!" she said with delight.

"Tracy, do you know anything about a list?"

"A list? No."

"Mmm. Okay."

After a moment of silence, Tracy said into the phone, "You doing okay?"

"Of course! I have a Sweet Pea snuggling next to me."

Tracy was tittering when we hung up. That was nice, to hear light laughter on such a dark day. I drew up a tentative plan in my head of how I intended to proceed in the Everybody Thinks I Murdered Whitney situation. If Rick wanted to augment his business by finding a way to build up his anemic snack counter, and Canine Confections was standing between him and high snack sales, it stood to reason he had something to lose by my being there. But even if he did want to ruin my business, what did he have against Whitney?

I thought about maybe checking that out. Then I thought about making a mug of hot cocoa with regular or mini-marshmallows, sitting in the deep cushions of the couch in my living room, and zoning out with the Cozi Channel. The *Andy Griffith Show*, maybe *Murder, She Wrote*. But a hot bath and sleep sounded better. The morning would come sooner than I thought.

I filled the marble tub with hot water, along with lavender aromatherapy salts and a glop of Mr. Bubble, and enjoyed an indulgent, delicious bath. Afterwards, I brushed my teeth and lowered the temperature on the air conditioner so I could enjoy the cozy comfort of my fuzzy socks and flannel pajamas without dying of heat stroke. I slipped on my favorite pjs and socks, and went to bed with my hand laying across Sweet Pea's torso. Glad I opted for a bath instead of staying up late watching TV, I sighed and snuggled into the blankets. I was feeling mostly safe and cozy, and hoped Sweet Pea felt the same—it had to be a big deal for her, her first night in a new home. I stroked her soft fur until finally, I drifted off to sleep and slipped into a dream where Andy Griffith and Jessica Fletcher were marching down the wedding aisle.

CHAPTER FOURTEEN

I had slept off and on all night. I'd dreamed Rick was standing next to my bed holding up a super-sized rawhide chew like he was going to crack me in the head with it, but as he swung it down, Rick morphed into Trumble. The detective was holding a bucket of fingerprint dust and interrogating me. He was also making fun of me in my flannel pajamas. "Don't you know we live in Florida?" he said. He crouched down to his knees—complaining the whole way down about his arthritis—pulled a rolling pin out from under my bed and dusted it for my prints. I cried, "Of course my fingerprints are on it, it's *my* rolling pin!" I woke up just as he was pulling out his handcuffs to drag me from my bed.

I wiped the sweat from my brow and shuffled into the kitchen, where I turned on the coffeepot and clipped the leash on to Sweet Pea's collar for a quick dash outside before our official morning walk. I made a mental note to ask Aunt Mary about the housekeeping and chef's schedule so I knew when it was safe to let Sweet Pea loose on the estate. While waiting for her to sniff what must have been a particularly interesting bush, I gazed up at the second floor of the Big House and imagined myself growing my hair long so I could Rapunzel my way out in case of fire. Sweet Pea and I returned to the cottage, and I fed her breakfast and drank my first cup of coffee while checking out Pinterest for fancy dog treats. By the time Sweet Pea finished her meal and I showered, I was wide awake and planning a new treat for every day of my grand opening week. I had already decided on the Creamy Cheese Drops for that day, but I hadn't yet decided if Fresh Carroty Cupcakes or Berry Delicious Melts would be better for the day after.

I quickly checked on my sleeping Aunt Mary and paused at the empty hangers in her closet. "That's strange," I said quietly to myself.

I drove toward Confections with Sweet Pea but when we reached the corner of South County Road and Worth Avenue, traffic on Worth was worse than I expected. A car behind us honked loudly.

Sweet Pea stuck her head out the passenger window.

"What's going on up there? Anything interesting?"

She didn't answer, only wiggled her nose in the air as we drove past Bottega Veneta, Hamilton Jewelers and Gucci. I raised the air conditioner since the cold air was blowing out her window. The closer I got to Canine Confections, the more cars honked and the more pedestrians strolled the sidewalk. Only they weren't strolling. They were walking really fast, not quite a jog, and their lips moved a million miles an hour.

A Honda Civic behind me laid on the horn. Poor Sweet Pea stuck her tail between her legs and made herself small in the passenger seat. I closed her window to keep the noise at bay.

If I thought I was going to find an empty parking space near Canine Confections, I was sadly mistaken. Driving five miles per hour, some of the walkers outpaced my car. Confections was only a couple stores up. By the time I reached Rick's Sophisticated Pet, people were speeding up.

Sweet Pea's curiosity must have overcome her fear. She peeked her head up from her seat, peered out the windows, and whined.

"It's okay, girl. It's just a little traffic ja—" and stopped mid-sentence in front of Canine Confections' large front display window.

Someone had written on top of the beautiful pink scroll with red spray paint. *Murder Site.*

CHAPTER FIFTEEN

My heart fell. Hot anger slowly burned its way up through my legs, torso, neck, face. I found a parking spot behind Confections and exited the car with Sweet Pea. I texted Tracy not to come through the front door, remembered that I hadn't committed to giving her a key, and realized I better make that decision sooner rather than later.

She texted back, "I'm here."

Her distressed face greeted me as soon as we entered from the back patio.

"I didn't want to clean off the graffiti until you saw it," she said, showing me a rag in her hand. "Mind if I get to it?"

I shoved the key in my pocket and unleashed Sweet Pea, who as usual greeted Tracy with happy whines and doggy licks. "How did you get in? I didn't give you a key."

"My friend stopped by yesterday while you were out so I asked her to get a copy made for me."

"What?"

She looked so stricken that I stopped.

"I didn't mean to make you mad," she said. "I was trying to be thoughtful. I thought it would save you the trouble of getting an extra made for me in case you wanted to give the second copy to your aunt."

"And you forgot to mention that to me?"

Her eyes welled up with tears.

Casually, I set my purse aside and asked, "Tracy, what kind of electives did you take back in school? Did they have cooking classes? Baking?"

She shook her head. "No, I took drawing."

"Right," I said with a nod. "How about drama? Were you ever in any plays? Have you done any acting?"

"No way! I would get stage fright if I had to be up on a stage in front of people!" she said and laughed.

I was interested to know if she had any acting ability. It would help me know how much of this airhead thing was an act. She had showed up a day early to my grand opening, told me everybody in town assumed I was to blame for Whitney's death, acted all happy-happy about helping me. *Got a key to my dog bakery made for herself.* I had to either trust her or not trust her. But were things really that black and white?

If she didn't work out, I would go back to the dreaded online interviews. It would be a long process doing background checks and asking the million questions I would have to ask someone I met online, but if that's what it took to find a dependable employee, I would do it. For now, I still had Tracy. What did she do that was so wrong? Make herself a key to save me the trouble? I was planning to give her one, anyway.

"This wasn't exactly what I had in mind for my second grand opening," I said, reaching into an upper cabinet and pulling out the silver platter I'd purchased for special events. I placed the Creamy Cheese Drops on it. Maybe not as prettily as Tracy would have done, but there wasn't much time.

"You're still doing the freebies?" Tracy asked.

"I may as well make the best of the situation. Look at all the free advertising I'm getting." Meanwhile, I'd check into Sexy Stubble about why he might want to kill Whitney and see if there was anything to Aunt Mary's mention of some kind of list.

"You mind?" Tracy dropped the rag. Her fingers started working their magic, arranging the Drops on the platter as if they were crystal droplets hanging from a chandelier.

Sweet Pea tilted her muzzle up to the platter.

"You're not getting a steady supply of treats." I split one in half, laid one half on a napkin behind the counter and popped the other half into Sweet Pea's mouth.

Tracy snickered. "You're really mistreating her … I can see the Humane Society calling now."

I cleaned off my hands and sighed. "Okay. I'm going to face the masses. Since you have the rag out, it *would* be great if you'd clean that off." I pointed at the red spray paint.

"No problem."

I held the platter and opened the front door. A small group of men and women milled about under Confections' canopy out on the sidewalk, and I took note of two men, one with a microphone, the other holding a video camera. On the camera's side, it said "Hot News Right Now."

CHAPTER SIXTEEN

"You didn't happen to see who wrote that, did you?" I asked a woman with wild, red hair and turquoise glasses. If she said a guy with a stubbly chin, I'd be disappointed, but better to find out now. She pretended she didn't see or hear me as she observed Tracy washing off the graffiti, then strolled with a group of women in the direction of Bebe and Patisserie, murmuring something about rolling pins.

"They're not making it easy on you, are they?" asked a man with a gorgeous golden retriever at his side.

"Nope."

The man with the mic shot in front of the camera. "This is Dick Jones with Hot News Right Now, your go-to for all the latest news in the hottest town in South Florida. We're here live with Samantha Armstrong, owner of Canine Confections on Worth Avenue." He shoved the mic in my face. "Miss Armstrong, how does it feel …" He fixed his gaze into the camera, then back at me, "for people to treat your new business like this?"

"Not too good, to be honest with you."

He nodded sympathetically. "Are you taking it personally?"

"It's hard not to," I said into his mic.

"You're new in town, aren't you?"

Not wanting to broadcast my entire life on local TV but also not wanting to cause a scene that would make it must-see TV, I said in what I hoped was a complete enough answer to satisfy him, "Yes."

He waited a moment while the cameraman panned the camera from us to Tracy cleaning off the graffiti, then returned to us. "Word is, it's one of the local shop owners that killed Whitney. So if not you, then who?"

"I have no idea."

"This isn't the type of thing Palm Beach is used to seeing. Do you think the residents feel your arrival coinciding with a murder is too big to ignore?"

I took a breath and talked into the camera. "I'm sure the residents here are smart enough to know that just because it happened in my dog bakery doesn't mean I had anything to do with it." I turned to the crowd and announced with my 110-watter smile, "Whoever has a dog, come on over. We have healthy, delicious Creamy Cheese Drops!"

The reporter's smile faded. I held the platter out and smiled at Tracy, who was wiping the remaining red paint off the window and slipping something into her back pocket.

The man with the golden sauntered up.

"What's her name?" I asked.

"Goldie."

"Hi, Goldie!"

I held the tray out for the owner, who lifted a Drop and offered it to her. She gobbled it up like a kid eating ice cream.

"She loves it!" he said.

Hot News murmured to each other's disappointed faces and left.

Soon, more early risers, canine and human, joined us. Now that the energy shifted from morose to celebratory, I invited everybody inside. Before I knew it, the place was buzzing. Success, thank goodness. *Aunt Mary, I am not losing your investment money.*

Sweet Pea tried to lick everyone who entered. I used my firm voice and miraculously, she learned to tune in to it very quickly. Every time she started to pad over to someone, unless they held their hand out, I told her, "Not yet," and then told her what a good girl she was. It worked like magic.

I had placed the tables further from each other than I normally would to allow plenty of space to keep everyone feeling safe and it seemed to be working. Everybody was smiling, including the dogs. Even Sweet Pea settled down and relaxed at all the action in what I was sure she already thought of as *her* dog bakery.

Tracy, on the other hand, was acting fidgety. I'd catch her watching me, then looking away. I sidled over to her at the sink next to the espresso machine. "What's the hub, bub?"

"Huh? Nothing. What do you mean?" she asked, all squirrely-like.

"Why are you acting so strange?"

She twisted her ponytail round and round in her index finger and chewed her lower lip. "I'm not acting strange."

I directed my gaze at her. I'd only known her two days. Maybe this was her normal behavior. "Tracy. What's going on?"

A bead of sweat dripped down the side of her cheek.

Martha strode in the front door. "Hello, all!" she said to anyone within hearing distance, which means … everybody in the café.

"Hi, Martha," I called out from behind the display case.

She grinned and said loudly on her way back to us, "I hear you had a little ruckus again this morning."

Tracy hightailed it away as Martha gave me a quick hug and murmured, "You poor thing."

"I guess you can call it that," I said. "But, and I don't mean to be rude … don't you have a pastry shop to run?"

Martha's smile faltered.

"God, I'm sorry," I said. "Is everything okay over there?"

"Yeah. Bethany is keeping an eye on it for me but I have to get back."

She didn't hurry off, though, so I tried to regain her good graces. "I really didn't mean to be rude." Very quietly, I said, "It's been a little nuts around here."

She nodded sympathetically.

"I don't know who spray-painted my window. I asked one of the women out front but she ignored me." I sliced a snip of lemon for an espresso cup plate.

Martha studied the espresso machine. "I haven't seen that model."

"My aunt splurged on the latest models of everything."

"You don't say?" Martha said. Her eyes had a faraway look for a moment. "I'm not surprised."

"At my aunt?" I was completely confused.

"Well, that," she said, confusing me even more. But before I had time to question it, she said, "I meant how rude that woman was who ignored you. Welcome to Palm Beach."

"Really? I know I haven't been here long, but so far most of the people have been pretty nice." Okay, not Bethany. And Rick was still to be determined.

We stared at the espresso dripping into its little cup.

"Think everybody will get bored and leave you alone soon?" she asked.

"I hope so."

I plated the espresso cup.

Martha smiled. "I love the smell of good coffee." Her eyes wandered to the display case. "And your goodies look good enough to eat!"

"For dogs only," I said.

Martha laughed and rushed out of Confections as quickly as she came in. As she turned to head back to Patisserie, the group with the redhead strolled past Confections again.

The bell on top of my door rang and two poodles—one standard, one toy—entered with two women. I recognized the older woman as Kristin Sullivan, a well-preserved woman in her seventies. She wore a delightfully brave outfit of an orange blazer over lime slacks and sat at a table with her much-younger friend and the two dogs at their feet.

"Welcome to Canine Confections," I said. "We have treats in the display case for the pups and espressos for their people."

Kristin ordered an espresso and an ice water. I hadn't intended to serve the tables, but I was a little on the desperate side of wanting to make Confections a success.

On my way to get their goodies, she said, "I'm glad we took the Bentley."

"I'm glad I took the Bentley" meant she didn't have her chauffer waiting in her antique Rolls-Royce on Worth Avenue. Kristin was still a girl who liked to gad about town, according to my aunt. The young lady at her side was probably Paulina, her personal assistant, much like Aunt Mary's Alice.

At the espresso machine, I mused on the unique traits of the affluent. I tugged the handle of the portafilter, the thing you put the coffee into—and didn't know my own strength. The portafilter flew into the air, over Goldie's retriever head, and landed at the standard poodle's paws.

I bolted over and since the dog was fine, I marveled at Kristin's ten-karat diamond ring. Now *there* was a prime example of conspicuous consumption. My aunt's lifestyle, aside from the mansion and estate, seemed almost quaint.

"I'm so sorry!" I said. "Is everybody okay?"

Paulina glowered at me, and for a moment I wasn't sure if she would answer or wrap her scarf around my neck and yank just for the fun of it. "You startled the dogs."

"Yeah. Sorry about that."

In a notch above a whisper, Kristin said, "Not the best start for you."

I couldn't tell if she was being kind or condescending. Since she opened the gate, I decided to take my opportunity. "I'll be fine once I get back on track," I assured her. "Once the police find out," I lowered my voice, "who murdered Whitney, everyone will move on."

"I hope so, for your sake."

I leveled my gaze at Kristin. "Did you know her?"

"I know her parents. The person you should be asking is Bethany. They were best friends all through school. Either that, or rivals. It's hard to keep it straight."

I left the women and poodles to their snacks, thinking that maybe I *should* talk to Bethany. According to the reporter, people thought it was one of the shop keepers. I needed to go by more than idle gossip, though. I checked the clock. It was still too early to expect Danny to be at the shelter and ask him about Whitney.

I wiped up the top of the display case even though it already gleamed and remembered that Rick was the one who might think of me as his competition. Maybe Bethany just hated the idea of dogs next to her art gallery *that* much? "Except why would she want to kill Whitney and hurt me?"

"Who?" Tracy said, suddenly at my side.

"What?"

"Why would *who* want to kill Whitney and hurt you?" Tracy asked.

"Oh. Bethany." I instantly regretted it. I had forgotten that fifteen minutes earlier Tracy was acting wonky. Now, she was at it again and I intended to get to the bottom of it.

"Bethany?" Tracy said loudly. The toy poodle barked.

A man stepped up to the display with his corgi. "Do you have anything nonfat?"

I gave Tracy a meaningful glance. She zipped her mouth shut.

"Most of what you see here is low in fat. I'd stay away from the cream cheese frosting if you want to keep your munchkin's weight down. What's her name?"

"*His* name is Snook'ums."

"Sorry. *His*. Hi, Snook'ums!" Snook'ums wagged his tail.

"Do you have anything here for people?" the man asked. "Pastry? Donut?"

"See?" Tracy called out as she slipped a fresh bag into the trash canister. "People want jelly donuts." She slammed the lid shut, which started a round of yaps from the small dogs in the café.

The man said quietly, "It doesn't have to be jelly."

"I know. Tracy is ... enthusiastic." I finished up with the man, wiped crumbs off a table and observed my new employee as I made my way over to the display counter. Tracy smiled at customers and their dogs as she whizzed past, and overall, was doing a fantastic job. When two women arrived at the counter, with no dog I might add, Tracy bolted over to it and almost ran into me in her haste. A notepad in her back pocket started to fall out, but I didn't tell her because by the time I picked up the handful of crumbs that had been in my hand, she was already at the register frowning at a pile of bills. The two women gave each other a sideways glance.

"Problem?" I asked.

They gave polite smiles and looked at Tracy, who said, "No. I'm just … not that good at math." She crammed the notepad deeper into her pocket, and we got the women settled with their money and espressos.

"Sorry," she said. "I got flustered. They gave me a fifty-dollar bill for two cups of espresso."

"We'll be cleaned out if that keeps happening." I needed to get to the bank. I would have loved to send Tracy but something told me that she would return with only half the money, a la George's uncle in *It's a Wonderful Life*. "Think you can hold things down while I run to the bank? It looks like the flood of customers has stopped." I pulled out the biggest bills from the register to get change. "If somebody wants to buy something, just tell them it's on the house. Make them feel special."

"Got it, boss," she said with a grin.

Sweet Pea peered up at me. "I'll be right back," I said to her and rubbed her little head.

I stepped out to the sidewalk and rubbed my eyes from the sudden blaze of sunshine. I didn't want to leave Tracy too long, but I heard soft laughter coming from Gallery Bebe's next door and wanted to strike while the iron was hot. Kristin mentioned that Bethany and Whitney had been friends throughout school but if that was true, Bethany wasn't spilling.

I squinted but the glare from the sun made it impossible to tell who was over there. All I could make out were two figures.

As I approached, Bethany and Martha were the two seated outside Gallery Bebe next to Palm Beach Patisserie, working on what appeared to be iced black coffees and a plate of mini-croissants. They looked up as I approached, and the sleeker of the two rose to her feet.

"Here to buy some art?" Bethany asked.

I gave them a smile a few degrees shadier than my sunniest. "Just stopping to say hello," I fibbed.

"Great!" Martha said. "We're all neighbors, right?"

"Like Mr. Roger's neighborhood," said Bethany. She paused and waited for my laugh.

I politely chuckled. "Your art gallery looks amazing, Bethany. I'd love to come in and look at your artwork sometime." It did, too: a black and white canopy hung over the door. Three pieces of contemporary art sat in the window. No price tags. Gold and silver confetti was casually spread around the art. Quite the sophisticated spread.

I glanced at Confections next door. Through the windows, customers sat and sipped. All of the dogs were lying down, except for the Aussie, who looked like he was dying to herd everyone.

"Those croissants look good, Martha. But I haven't been able to regain my appetite since yesterday morning." I meant it to steer the conversation to the murder, which it did.

"Shocking thing about Whitney," Martha said. "Really shocking."

"It's awful," Bethany said in an arrogant voice. "It makes you look at other people with new eyes—wondering."

"Could you tell me the last time you saw Whitney?"

They looked at each other. Then Martha replied:

"Let's see ... It was two nights ago, the evening before you found her at Confections. We closed Patisserie and left around six. Is that about when you waved good-bye to us, Bethany?"

Bethany nodded.

I fiddled with the string on my trousers and asked nonchalantly, "Was anyone else around?"

"Sure," Martha said. "There's usually *someone* on this street."

"Late-afternoon shoppers," Bethany said. "Shopkeepers closing up. But I don't remember seeing anyone loitering in the area."

At least not that evening. But Bethany had told me she saw Rick wandering around earlier than usual the following morning, which was yesterday, the morning of my grand non-opening.

"I don't think I remember anyone either," said Martha hesitantly. "Whitney and I left Patisserie together. I asked her if she wanted to go to dinner. She told me she hoped it got chilly later that evening because she wanted to sit out in her yard and have a brandy with her parents and their chihuahua to see if the little dog would acclimate okay to Sweet Pea in her house."

Chilly on a summer evening in Florida. *Good luck.* "And neither of you saw anything odd?" I pressed.

"No," they said in unison.

"Have either of you noticed any strangers prowling around? Anyone who apparently doesn't belong on Worth Avenue?"

Bethany looked me up and down.

"Really?" I said.

"I'm only teasing."

Martha scowled. "Yes. She's only *teasing*."

"Lighten up, you two," Bethany said. "We welcome outsiders all the time."

"As long as they have a few million in their bank account, right, Bethany?" Martha asked.

I couldn't tell what was going on. If these two were friends or frenemies or simply new business neighbors.

Bethany twisted a napkin between her long, graceful fingers. "If you mean, have we seen anyone wearing a trench coat and dark sunglasses, I'll say no. I haven't noticed anyone who even *remotely* resembles a villain. You, Martha?"

"Can't say that I have."

I wanted to dive in and ask them about Rick. I also wanted to ask Bethany about what Kristin said in regard to them being best friends in school. "I'm surprised Patisserie is open with Whitney gone."

Martha picked at a croissant. "With all the work Whitney did, no one wanted to see it all go to waste by closing it after only a week."

The dark circles under her eyes brought up a few questions. "It must be hard on you," I said. "Are you running it all by yourself?"

Martha shrugged. "She was a sweet girl."

Bethany sniggered.

"She *wasn't* sweet?" I asked.

Bethany tossed the subject aside with a slight shrug. "Martha's looking a little rough around the edges because of all that dancing she's been doing."

"Dancing?" I asked.

Martha said, "A place over in West Palm."

She didn't strike me as the dancing type. "What kind of music?"

"It's called Latin Forever, so figure it out," said Bethany.

"It's in my neighborhood," shrugged Martha, which meant she was the only one on our little strip of Worth who didn't live in Palm Beach.

I took the plunge. "What do you guys think of the neighbors around here?" I asked.

They both stared at me like I had lost my mind.

"Oka-aay," I tried, "Did Whitney complain of anything?" I held three fingers up in the Girl Scout Promise. "Any accusation you make won't go past this slab of sidewalk. Promise."

Martha offered, "She accused one of her new steady customers of wearing last year's shoes. But that's hardly criminal. No, to the best of my knowledge everyone in the area liked Whitney—you and she were best friends pretty much, right, Bethany?"

Bethany's face shaded pink. Meaning both Tracy and Lime Slacks had told me the truth.

Amy Hueston | 137

"We're not much help, are we?" Martha said.

Bethany took a sip of her iced coffee and tore a tiny corner off of a croissant, allowing me a moment to eyeball her directly. I wondered not for the first time, if she and I would become friends. I hoped so, but I wouldn't hold my breath.

I threw her a softball to help her backpedal her insinuation that she and Whitney were mere neighbors on Worth Avenue. "You and Whitney were pretty good friends, then?"

She peered up at me through her thick lashes. "Her group was into parties and hooking up with the hottest guys back in high school. My group was interested in culture. The latest exhibits at the Norton Museum, like that."

"Hence you opening up an art gallery."

"Mmmm. *Hence.*"

"Oh, come on," Martha prodded. "You and Whitney did more than run in different circles. She said you two had a full-blown rivalry since kindergarten!"

Kristin had used the word rivals to discuss the two women, too.

Bethany asked, "Are we here to talk about my childhood or are we trying to find out what happened to Whitney?"

"Did you and Whitney have a rivalry?" I asked.

"I'm not sure you'd call it a rivalry. Occasionally, there was a guy we both liked but usually not at the same time." She lowered her chin to the iced coffee in front of her. "This was back in junior high, mind you.

By the time we'd reached high school, our tastes drastically changed direction."

The longer Bethany talked, the more Martha's lips twitched in a smile.

"What did Whitney used to say?" I asked Martha. To Bethany, "You don't mind, right?"

"Why would I mind an interrogation from the new girl in town?"

"Oh, good. Martha?"

Martha explained, "Whitney and I talked a lot, especially to pass the time while we cleaned up crumbs from all the uppity customers."

"Uppity?"

"You'll see. Anyway, we didn't have much time together since Patisserie has only been open for a week."

"Yeah. I thought that was strange that it opened only a week before Confections," I said.

Bethany offered, "The town has been busy doing renovations and letting all kinds of new stores open." From the look on her face, I didn't think Bethany was too thrilled about this.

Martha slugged her iced coffee. "Whitney snagged this place a few weeks ago."

"What do you mean snagged it?" I asked.

"I mean her mommy and daddy bypassed all the other people on the list who were hoping to get dibs on this space," Martha said.

So Aunt Mary was right on the mark.

Bethany tore the remains of her mostly untouched croissant and stared straight at me. "Maybe everybody is right," she said. "You're the one who should be questioned. All these years Whitney has lived here, she's been fine. Then boom, *you* move to town and she winds up dead."

"Bethany!" Martha said.

"What, she can interrogate me like I'm a common criminal and I have to sit here and take it?"

"I'm sorry if you feel I was interrogating you but I had nothing to do with Whitney's murder." I settled my eyes on the sidewalk and after a moment, glanced up at her. "Do you know who had something to gain by killing Whitney and leaving her in my dog bakery?"

Bethany shook her head. "Again I ask, what makes you think the world revolves around you and that the two are connected?"

"Good point," Martha said.

"So, you think Whitney and whoever killed her were in my dog bakery for another reason and got in a fight at the last minute?"

Bethany pondered that for a moment. "Maybe. I really don't know."

"I can't imagine," Martha said and stuffed the remainder of a chocolate croissant into her mouth.

"The only one I can think of that had something to gain is Rick," said Bethany.

Martha bobbed her head up and down and swallowed. "Yeah! He has that little counter by the cash register where he sells a couple of dog snacks. Maybe he didn't like you coming in to his territory."

Bethany snickered. "See?" she said to me. "What did I tell you?"

"*You* told me I was making this all about me," I said.

"I also told you I saw him hanging around the morning Whitney was found and maybe he was sizing up the competition. I mean, you do know he sells dog snacks, right?" She shrugged. "It doesn't mean I think he's a murderer."

"Doesn't mean he isn't," Martha said cheerfully.

Bethany looked at her aghast.

"What? I'm just kidding! Lighten up, you two!" Martha popped another bite of croissant into her mouth.

I asked them, "Did he have anything against Whitney?"

Bethany shook her head, but Martha took a moment to swallow and offered, "She told me he asked her out a bunch of times, but she wasn't interested. She seemed a little scared, maybe?"

"Scared?" I asked. "Of Rick?"

"She told you that?" Bethany asked Martha.

Martha split a brand-new croissant in half, took a bite and nodded.

"Why would she be scared of Rick?" I asked.

When they both responded with nothing more than a shrug, I said no more. They each gave me things to consider but I still needed to feel them out. If one or the other of them wanted to believe they'd snookered me, so much the better.

I slipped my sunglasses on. "If you hear anything, pop on over."

They might be polite, offering me iced coffees, warm croissants and what-not, but I thought Martha and Bethany's niceties were dubious. I pledged they would never get my votes for Palm Beach's Welcoming Committee's Most Sincere.

What had I learned so far? Well, for one thing, Bethany knew Whitney more than she let on. That was already implied not only by Tracy, Aunt Mary, Kristin and Martha but by Bethany herself. It's hard to fight a red face. Two, Aunt Mary was right about there being a list, too, a list that went by the wayside when Whitney's parents used their influence. Three, Rick, who already sold dog snacks and maybe envisioned expanding his snack product line, was the only other business that had something to lose by Canine Confections' presence on Worth. And he had been scaring Whitney by his advances and then showed up early the morning of her murder.

There was no way I was going to let this continue and ruin my business. Aunt Mary loaned me the money for Canine Confections with no pressure to return her investment, but that made it all the more important. My sweet aunt was not going to lose a *dime* on *my* watch. And not only because if she lost her money it meant I'd be pretty much out on the street far as I was concerned. I wasn't about to become a loser relative crashing on my aunt's couch, even if she did own four rooms of them.

I thanked them for their cooperation—vague though it was—and warned I might return with more questions. They couldn't have been more genial, but when I ambled down the street, I heard their muted laughter drifting down the sidewalk.

CHAPTER SEVENTEEN

My next stop was the bank, and then casually walking past Sophisticated Pet. But since I'm not a fan of breakfast and it was growing near one in the afternoon, I ducked back into Confections to give Tracy a lunch break and grab the lunch I'd brought from home. The crowd inside had dwindled to almost nothing. Sweet Pea wagged her tail at my arrival, and a fifty-something year-old man with a goatee idly sat in the cafe with his cocker spaniel.

"Hi, honey!" I said to the golden bundle of fur on my way to the display counter. She lifted her head, then set it back down onto her paws.

Tracy dried her hands and looked at me expectantly. "Do you want me to put the change in the drawer?"

"I haven't made it to the bank yet."

"Oh?"

I liked the girl but, as with Martha and Bethany, I didn't know her yet. No need to fill her in on my questioning of them.

Softly, I asked, "Did you give him something on the house?"

"Yeah. He got a Carob Cookie. He wanted to pay but I told him we were having a special."

"Thanks." I looked around the mostly empty dog bakery. "I see we lost everybody else and no one new came in?"

"Yeah. Sorry. I overhead some customers talking and they said mostly everybody came in just to see the murder site, and they probably wouldn't be back anytime soon."

Alright, well that was no fun to hear.

I sighed. "So, you ready to take a lunch break?"

"What about him?" She whispered and gestured to Goatee.

Maybe his ears burned because he got up and headed for the door. "Thank you! Jasper loved the cookie."

"Come back soon!" Tracy said with almost too much glee.

"I brought my lunch from home. I'll go to the bank after you return."

"I brought mine too!" Tracy said with an enthusiasm usually reserved for climbing on the horsey on a Merry-Go-Round.

My craving for the avocado and tomato on the homemade, whole-grain bread Aunt Mary's Chef Luca baked from scratch could not be denied a moment longer. I rushed past Tracy and pulled it out of the refrigerator in the back, along with an iced-cold lemonade. Sweet Pea tap-danced.

"You wouldn't like it," I told the furball. "Too many vegetables."

"I'm going to eat lunch in the café," Tracy said and grabbed her yogurt from the frig. "I like to people-watch while they pass on the sidewalk."

Sandwich and a notepad in hand, I strolled around the small patio out back where I had planted a few dwarf palms to cozy up the place. Next, I scribbled notes about my conversation with Martha and Bethany and thought about how Martha said Whitney was scared of Rick. Next, I googled Tracy again. Not because I didn't trust her. Actually, that was exactly why I googled her. Nothing popped up but a few short stories in *Pulse on Palm Beach*.

I called the shelter. "Hi. Can I speak with Danny, please?"

"He's feeding the dogs," the woman said at the other end of my phone.

It was just as well. I wanted to see him face to face when I asked about Whitney. "How late can I come see him?"

"He's here until five."

I thanked her, pressed End on my cell, and went back inside.

I filled Sweet Pea's bowl with fresh water and clicked her leash onto her collar. "You're a busy girl!" I told her. Tracy was deep in cell phone land in the café. "No people for you to watch?"

"I guess it's too humid out."

"You okay for another few minutes while I go to the bank?"

She gestured to the empty sidewalk and grinned. "Pretty sure."

Sweet Pea and I strolled down Worth, peering into store windows to see how the rest of the stores were doing in the middle of the humid day. The humidity pressed down on me. I knew my hair must be a mass of frizz. Once I had gotten enough distance from Confections, a slow but steady stream of customers in their South Florida corals, light blues and citrusy greens strolled along the Avenue. Inside the shops they perused through clothing racks, paid for wares and entered and exited the doors. Plenty of dogs padded past too, yet after our initial onslaught of customers that morning, we had nary a one.

The redhead from earlier strolled past and threw me a nice smile like we were happy acquaintances. Maybe she really *hadn't* heard me ask her about the spray paint earlier.

Sweet Pea and I entered Rick's store two minutes later.

Rick was on the phone with a Mont Blanc pen in his hand. He was poring over a crossword puzzle, a man after my own heart. "I was told I would be next on the list," he said to somebody on the phone, not noticing we had come in. "Why did that not happen?" He listened to the person at the other end of his cell and hung up.

Sweet Pea and I moseyed over to him at the counter. She tugged on her leash to say hello.

"Rough day?" I asked politely. "Your face is a little redder than I remember."

He eased the tension from his jaw. "Supplier is late getting me the dog sweaters I ordered. Said they're backed up." Rick shook his head. "He promised me I'd be the first to get them when they came in."

I gestured to the Mont Blanc in his hand. "Is it true that expensive pens only give the right words when you do a crossword puzzle?"

Sexy Stubble grinned, leaned over and petted my girl's fluffy face. "She this friendly with everyone?"

"Pretty much. Sorry." I swiveled my head around his mostly empty store.

"You just missed the rush," he said.

"I thought maybe we were all slow."

"Because of the murder?"

His words, so cold and harsh, fit the image that was beginning to grow that he was someone to watch out for. The only one with something to lose by my dog bakery being here, plus unrequited feelings for Whitney … unless you count Bethany's general disdain for dogs and her frenemy relationship with Whitney. My feeling upon seeing him was, not terror, but … trepidation.

At least a few inches taller than my 5'5", with blue eyes that were as pretty as Aunt Mary's and so much prettier than my brown ones, his hair fell across the top of his forehead, and his smile could make millions for Crest.

"Now that you brought it up, how well did you know Whitney?" I asked. Nothing like jumping into the deep end of a pool without knowing if the other swimmers are going to drown you.

"You get right to the point, don't you?" he said without answering my question. "She was in the same grade as me, but we didn't have many classes together."

"When is the last time you saw her?"

"There are a lot more pleasant ways to interrogate me."

Interrogate. Same word Bethany used.

"Do tell." Flirting or not, I wanted the answer. I placed a smile on my face and kept it there, but my lips remained closed.

He sighed and seemed to think about it before answering. "I probably saw her the day before she died."

"Probably?"

He pressed his lips together and squinted at me. I could tell I'd almost reached my quota of pressing questions. "Definitely. She only opened Palm Beach Patisserie a week ago. I went by every day to show support to an old friend."

"An old friend."

"More like old classmates. We were in the same grade in school." He drew circles with his pen on the side of his crossword. "I stopped and got a piece of crumb cake every morning to give her the business."

Not according to his flat abdomen.

Rick grinned ... I had been staring at his stomach. "If I killed Whitney, do you think Sweet Pea would be so friendly to me?" His smile slid into a sexy half-smile. "I was helping her business out, like I'd do for you. We're all neighbors here."

Only so far, he hadn't dropped by Confections except for yesterday morning. "I've already seen Martha and Bethany several times since yesterday."

"Bethany," he said with a little chuckle.

"What's wrong with Bethany?"

"Nothing. She and Whitney were the head of their two different cliques back in school. Both cliques equally snobby. Why do girls have to be like that?"

"School was many years ago."

In mock concern, he asked, "Is my hair turning gray already?"

"Is there anyone around that you think might have wanted Whitney dead? Or wanted to hurt my business? Or both?"

"What?"

I hadn't intended to come out and tell him my suspicions like that but on the other hand, I thought catching him on the fly might be a good idea.

"Is this because the police came around and questioned all of us about you?" he asked.

His hands twirled around the pen hovering above his crossword puzzle, and his lips twitched in an almost-smile. I still hadn't figured him out. *Why was everybody acting so silly and cavalier about a dead woman?*

"Don't worry," he said. "I told the police I thought you were innocent."

I chewed the inside of my mouth and pondered my next question while I checked out the snacks. "What are these, peanut butter?"

"Yeah. And carob."

"Nice."

Sweet Pea peeked up at me.

"You mind?" Rick asked as he pulled a treat out of the glass case.

"Only a corner of one. She had enough this morning."

Sweet Pea licked his hand with as much zest as Tracy helping me at Confections.

"Okay, girl," I said. "He doesn't need a bath."

Sweet Pea chewed while I considered my next question. I could only go down this road for so long before he kicked me out of his store. "Some of the people around here think leaving Whitney's body on my floor was a sure way to hurt my business."

"If somebody wanted to hurt your business, there are easier ways than killing someone and leaving the dead body in your shop." He said this with such surety that it made me wonder if he had personal experience with this sort of thing.

"Like what?"

He wiped his hands of crumbs and pet Sweet Pea's forehead. "I don't know. Burn the place down." Under his breath, he said, "But then the other stores in the area would be ruined, too." Excited, he raised his index finger in the air, "They could have just killed *you*!"

Rick said this with such merriment, that I stepped back on instinct.

He let out a big laugh. "Am I freaking you out? I just like to solve puzzles." He lifted the crossword puzzle on the counter as solid proof.

I leaned down and petted Sweet Pea while I gathered my thoughts.

Rick seemed eager to help and excited by the whole thing. "It could be me, of course. But then, you've already thought of that."

150 | Paws for Concern

I peered up and he peered right back. The bit of smile on his lips reached his eyes. If he was the murderer, he had to be a sociopath, because he was exceptional at hiding his guilt.

Rick began making squares with his Mont Blanc all over the crossword puzzle page. "Of course, like you said earlier, killing Whitney and leaving her in your dog bakery takes care of both problems. You *and* Whitney. Who had it in for both of you?" he asked like I would know.

"I have no idea. I just moved here a month ago."

"Right. How's that going?"

"Let's stay on the subject."

"Okay." Pen to cleft chin, he said, "Murder, murder … how about friends from her past? Old boyfriends?"

Getting Martha in trouble by telling him Whitney said he scared her was no better than getting Bethany in trouble for saying he was walking around that morning. "Have you ever asked Whitney out?"

"No. She wasn't my style."

Which meant Martha had it wrong. Either that, or Rick was lying. Or, *Whitney* had lied.

Sweet Pea tugged on the leash and made nice with Rick. "You're not getting any more treats right now," I said to the little beggar. "We're going to have to start taking longer jogs if you're going to be around snacks so often."

Rick laid the pen on the counter and kneeled to pet the girl. "You're pretty darn cute." He rubbed Sweet Pea's face and chest and looked up at me. "If you start taking longer walks and she gets sore, I sell arnica and some other homeopathic remedies."

I followed his gaze to an aisle filled with bottles and jars. "I love that! I use organic ingredients in my bakery items."

While Rick smiled and snuggled with Sweet Pea, I ran through the short list of questions one more time with meager results. Yes, he had seen Whitney the day before she died. That was the last time he had seen her. No, he did not believe anyone on Worth Avenue was capable of murder. And while he had seen no strangers lollygagging about, it was his theory that a madman must have killed Whitney and left her corpse in my dog bakery. Always game for a puzzle, the close proximity of the murder had given him the willies. But it also seemed like fun to figure out.

I listened to him, hearing every word, but the looky-loos outside Sophisticated Pet's window distracted me more than it should. A man and woman were gesturing to me, then pointing down the block in the direction of Canine Confections.

"You're the talk of the town," Rick said.

"I hoped it would be because Confections was a huge hit."

"I tried my hand at it." He gestured to the two different snacks in his case. "I didn't get very far. Starbucks down the block gives free whipped cream. The dogs are happy enough with that."

He raised his hands up at my scathing look. "Don't kill the messenger!"

I gathered Sweet Pea's leash. "I'm a little on edge," I said hastily. "Dead body in my dog bakery, you know." I laughed lightly but it came out in a tinnier tone than I'd hoped.

"I didn't mean anything by it. Just me running my mouth again," Rick said.

By the time I was out the door, he was gripping the Mont Blanc to get back to his crossword.

I left Rick's store, disappointed that instead of gaining clarity, I was only *more* suspicious of my fellow shop owners. It reminded me of throwing spaghetti on a kitchen cabinet and seeing which one stuck—my cabinets were covered with spaghetti strands. I dashed over to the bank, then back to Canine Confections, where Tracy was playing with the layout of the tables in the café.

"I love how you placed them to make it cozy," I said, "but I want to give the dogs plenty of space from other dogs."

"Okay," she said and shoved the tables back.

We spent the rest of the afternoon reviewing how to handle the cash register when she gets overwhelmed and discussing things like the placement of our Specials of the Day sign: Centered in the display case, inside the display case …? We voted to put it on top of the display case.

By the time we finished, it was almost five o'clock. We hadn't had any customers all afternoon.

"I think they're freaked out," Tracy said.

I shook my head at a tiny red smudge still on the front window. "I didn't realize you didn't get all that off." Jumping up and grabbing a rag and a bottle of Windex, I exited the front door and tried scrubbing it off the glass, but it was pretty stubborn. Sweet Pea's tongue lolled out the side of her mouth at me from inside Confections. The more I scrubbed, the more frustrated I grew. Bethany and Martha caught sight of me and I was pretty sure they were laughing. Or maybe I was being paranoid and seeing enemies everywhere.

Tracy joined me. "Let me do that."

"Thanks."

I left her to finish while I straightened my desk in the back room and checked out the walk-in refrigerator and dry goods walk-in. After a few minutes, Tracy returned and we closed up shop. I'd done enough sleuthing for one day, and besides, asking the same questions continually had the same effect as banging my head against a concrete wall, including the headache. My last bit of digging was to stop at the shelter to talk to Danny in case he had something fascinating to report about Whitney. But I wasn't getting my hopes up.

Tracy and I said our good-byes and Sweet Pea happily jumped into the car. We drove down Worth Avenue and over to the shelter, where I pulled into the parking lot and paused while I decided if I wanted to subject Sweet Pea to recognizing the scents of the place she had lived.

"That is a big no," I said. I played with my keys outside my car of the parking lot, not wanting to bring her inside thinking I was returning her but not willing to leave her in the car. As I mulled it over, the bright idea of my cell phone crossed my brain. I made the call and said, "I'm outside in your parking lot and I know you might think I'm crazy but I have my ..." All of a sudden, I remembered that Sweet Pea wasn't officially, legally mine yet. I didn't know for sure if the Goodwins signed the paperwork, but chances were very good they hadn't gotten around to it yet.

I panicked, thinking the good people of the shelter might recognize Sweet Pea, remember I wasn't the woman who had adopted her—especially when I was here to ask about that woman—and take her from me to give back to her "rightful owner." I hung up the phone, jumped back in my car, slammed the door and squealed out of the parking lot like I was in a car chase with the police on my tail.

Sweet Pea glanced at me and back out the window.

"Great," I said to myself. "Now if I call they won't *think* I'm crazy, they'll be *sure* of it. And worse, I still haven't asked them about Whitney."

It didn't matter what the shelter thought about me. And Sweet Pea was safely gone from their parking lot. It's not like they were going to send anyone for her.

I called back as I drove home to Whitehall. "Sorry," I said. "Must have been a bad connection. Can I talk to Danny?"

A disinterested female voice said, "Sure."

I glimpsed at Sweet Pea.

"I was told you are the one who adopted Sweet Pea out to Whitney?"

"Yeah, why?"

"Anything you can tell me about her?"

"No."

We arrived at Aunt Mary's gate. I pressed the code and since Danny was far from chatty, I threw out my planned chatter about "she must have seemed excited about getting a new dog" out the window. The gate opened and I drove past the Big House to the cottage, then got right to the point.

"Aside from the obvious excitement of adopting a dog, did she say anything unusual?" I asked.

I exited the car and opened the cottage door for Sweet Pea.

"Like what?"

"Anything about being scared, maybe? Was she talking on the phone at all while she was there?"

"Lemme think ..."

I let him think but as I am wont to do, got impatient. "Did she say anything about being happy about some kind of list?" I didn't want to feed the guy answers but, laconic as *he* was, it didn't seem much of a concern.

Sweet Pea ran inside. I laid my purse on the kitchen table, refreshed her water bowl and poured myself a glass of water, then gazed at the palm tree outside the front window.

"No, nothing about a list. But she answered her cell while I was at the front desk. She was telling whoever was on the other end of the phone that she would prove to everyone that she could run a business as well as her."

"Who?"

"Huh?"

"Who is *her*?"

"Oh. No idea."

If the *her* in question was Bethany, then once again the trail led to the art gallery owner, innocuous or not.

When no other information proved interesting, I thanked Danny, hung up, threw on my bathing suit, and left Sweet Pea snoozing in the air conditioning in the cottage while I went down to the beach for a swim. I swam for my ten minutes straight and returned home in time for cocktail half-hour with Aunt Mary (seltzer and a slice of orange), dinner and tv, and snuggle-time with the girl.

By nine o'clock that evening, I set the air conditioning to freezing, pulled on my coziest pajamas and turned out the light. My closet door stood open, my favorite little black dress seeming to mock me. I wouldn't have minded a date with somebody nice, but at the moment, I was so exhausted and depleted from the grand opening, the murder, and the emotional highs of my new dog that I was thrilled to be exactly where I was. By the looks of Sweet Pea's muzzle firmly in the palm of my hand, the feeling seemed to be mutual.

Unfortunately, the following morning ushered in a new dose of trouble.

CHAPTER EIGHTEEN

Sweet Pea and I came over to check on Aunt Mary, who was on the phone in the library. Hearing the strain in her voice, I stopped a few feet from the threshold.

"But where will I live?" she asked.

A moment later, she sniffled and hung up.

Where will she live?

Sweet Pea wasn't great at being sneaky. She chuffed and ran into the library and over to Aunt Mary. I followed her into the room and stopped when Aunt Mary wiped her eyes with a tissue.

"Oh, good morning, honey," she said.

"What's going on?"

She stood up slowly from her chair, babying her knee for once.

"Hold on," I said and ran for her cane.

Several tears ran down her cheek. "I didn't mean for you to see me like this." She leaned on her cane as we all made our way out of the library and towards the kitchen. "It's Matthew."

"Who?"

"My financial advisor." She walked with the cane, leaning down every time the weight came down on her left leg. "Uncle Joseph never wanted to talk to me about our investments. He only told me I'd be taken care of. But Matthew said aside from the house—"

"You mean this house, right?"

She nodded. "Yes. Aside from this, we only had that money I invested in your …" She cut herself off.

In a panic, I met her eyes. "You mean …" I started. "The rest of your life savings is invested in Canine Confections?"

I began to hyperventilate and paced up and down the hall as we made the long journey from library to kitchen.

"See?" she said. "This is what I was afraid of. I didn't want to tell you."

"Didn't your financial investor tell you this when you told him you were giving me money?"

"He said that he did but that I wouldn't listen. Which *does* sound like me …"

"I'll give it back! We'll get our money back from the commercial realtor. I'll call Gabriella!"

She shook her head. "It's too late. My word is my bond. I'm not backing out of the agreement with the realtor and I'm not backing out of my agreement with you."

"But I don't know if Confections will even succeed. With the murder—"

"What kind of language is that coming from you? Since when do *you* lack the confidence to press forward?"

Finally, we reached the kitchen. I settled Aunt Mary in a chair and opened the back door for Sweet Pea. "What do you mean? If I had the confidence, I wouldn't have been working in somebody else's bakery in Sun Haven."

I filled two cups with coffee and placed them on saucers, then joined my aunt at the table.

"Are you forgetting that I know why you hadn't yet opened your own dog bakery there?" she asked kindly.

"Because I never got around to it," I said, purposely looking anywhere but at my aunt.

"Nonsense. You graduated college and were ready to get your own business off the ground, and you put it off to work as many hours as you could to help your parents during the mortgage crisis." My aunt shook her head. "If I had only known, but my brother is a stubborn one—"

"Gee, it must run in the family—"

"And I didn't find out about his money problems until your Uncle Joseph and I returned from Switzerland or Monaco or wherever we were."

"My parents are fine. They still have their house. Everything is good. They're on a cruise right now. And not the kind of cruise people take because it's the cheapest way to take a vacation ... they're on a *river* cruise. In Europe."

"And all that time you would have spent on establishing your business was spent working extra hours at Debbie's Bakery."

I shifted in my chair. "You're making my parents sound like awful people."

"I don't mean to. It's just ... life got in the way. They're good people, your parents."

"Yes. They are."

She opened her arms wide. "And now, look! You're here taking care of me."

"I wouldn't call giving you an ice pack twice a day taking care of you."

"You do more than that. And I won't let you give up your dreams again. I'll lose this house before I do that."

She could say what she wanted, but I'd never let that happen. That was why this had to work. I could see it now, Confections fails, my aunt loses her money, I run off without telling her where I am because she would spend her last penny on me, and I'd feel worse than ever.

"I have a picture in my head ..." I began.

She looked me in the eye. "Yes?"

I didn't tell her the scary picture in my head, the one where I'm living on the streets and afraid to call her because I didn't want her to rescue me. I shared the happy picture. "Yes. It's of you, me and Sweet Pea, happily eating cupcakes with fresh whipped cream, laughing, and your knee is better than it ever was ... in fact, you're considering entering the Senior Olympics!"

Aunt Mary laughed and sipped. "Is there such a thing?"

I shrugged. "I don't know. If there isn't, there should be."

We sat in silence for a moment.

She said, "You do more for me than give me an ice pack. You bring in my mail, serve me meals—"

"Chef Luca prepares your meals ahead of time." Like a flashlight beaming into my head, I said, "Is that why he only comes three times a week now? Because you couldn't afford him every day?"

She waved me away. "I've sold some of my clothes to a consignment shop ..."

"Excuse me? You did what?"

"To make a few extra dollars. What do I need with all of those designer clothes in my closet?"

A heat rose in my face. I wrapped my hand around the cup so the warmth could calm me. "Things are that bad that you're selling your clothes?"

Aunt Mary chuckled. "You make it sound like I have nothing but tee shirts left. My dear, many of my clothes cost thousands of dollars for one item."

A world I never experienced firsthand.

She sipped her coffee. "I still have plenty left in my closet. I do miss a small brooch I gave to a shop. They said they sold it already for a bargain. But if you see anyone wandering around town with a brooch and a large M for Mary, let me know." She laughed to make light.

A half hour later, I drove down Ocean Boulevard with Sweet Pea in the passenger seat, my jaw set in grim determination to make Confections succeed if I had to pick every peanut myself for the peanut butter. Sweet Pea's ears flew in the wind from the open window. I crossed Royal Palm Way, past tall edifices of glass and stainless steel. The gleaming modernism contrasted with Sun Haven like a frog sitting next to an ant.

My cell rang in my lap.

"It's Trumble. Mind coming by?"

"I'm on my way to work …"

"I can come there if you prefer."

I envisioned another day of police and detectives at Confections. "Can it wait until noon so I can get things rolling before I leave it to my new employee?"

"If you mean Tracy Oshkosh, she's why I'm contacting you."

My stomach squelched.

"Sure. I can stop by."

"Thought you might change your mind."

Five minutes later, I was squirming in a large leather chair in the foyer of the police department with Sweet Pea lying on the floor next to me.

Sweet Pea jumped up and licked Trumble's hand so profusely that the detective grabbed a box of tissues off the front desk. He led us back to his office for the second time in as many days.

In his office, he said, "Take a seat."

"You mean *have* a seat, right?" I couldn't help myself.

"You being smart?"

I felt a little smile start to creep up my lips.

"Are you amused?"

Aside from moving to a new town, opening up a dog bakery where a dead body was lying on the floor, and a detective calling me all the time? No, not amused. Just giddily unnerved.

I shook my head and held my palms up in surrender. "I'm not trying to give you trouble, I promise. I'm a little overwhelmed, that's all."

"That girl you got working for you. Tracy. How well do you know her?"

"I just met her two days ago."

"I know you left her when the locksmith was coming, but word on the street is you're leaving her alone in your new business establishment. That seem wise to you?"

I shifted in my seat. Sweet Pea moved from one haunch to the other at my feet.

"You aware that Tracy Oshkosh is a leading suspect in a crime?"

Tracy? I should have known better, I know, but the girl was as far from a criminal as a Devil Dog is to real food.

"Where is she? Do you have her here now?"

"We had to let her go for now."

Since when did Trumble keep me in the loop on criminal suspects?

"Why did you want to talk to me? What did she do?" I asked.

"Palm Beach Patisserie had a break-in last night."

"Whitney's pastry shop?"

"Martha's been taking over while Whitney's parents decide what to do with it. She said she saw Tracy throw a rock at the back door and run away. She forgot her car keys inside Patisserie. Tracy must have thought she was gone for the evening, maybe planned to steal some recipes, and Martha caught her in the act."

"Have you checked Martha out? That doesn't sound like Tracy."

The folds in Trumble's cheeks increased when he grimaced. "Maybe don't tell me how to do my job. I don't care whose niece you are." He paused for effect. "Like I said, how well do you know her?"

I thought about the notepad in her pocket, and how she stuck it back there in a flash whenever I came into the room. *Was she trying to make it with Pulse on Palm Beach by breaking a story on me?*

Under the shame, I felt a disappointment that didn't make sense. I must have been more desperate for an employee and a friend than I thought.

"I hear you've been digging on your own," Trumble said.

"Where did you hear that?"

"It's a small town." His hazel eyes held a keen intelligence.

I gave him the names of the few people I'd talked with on Worth Avenue. I recited the gist of the conversations I had with Bethany Westwood, Martha Crenshaw and Rick Newman. I described their shops and told him their demeanors all seemed normal. *Mostly.*

He scribbled rapid notes on his pad and when I finished, he looked up at me suspiciously. "And that's all you have?"

"That's it."

"Don't mean to be rough on you, but something tells me you got something else." I knew I wasn't wrong about those eyes.

"I'm pretty sure it's nothing."

"I'll let you know if it's nothing or not."

"Bethany, the owner of Gallery Bebe ... she fibbed to me."

"Fibbed?"

"Lied."

"A lot of people lie. It's one reason I called you in, instead of telling you about Tracy over the phone."

I sat up taller in my chair. "Excuse me?"

"It's easier to lie over the phone. I wanted to see your face. Normally, I like to keep things closer to the vest but I got a feeling about you. I think you're probably okay."

"I feel all warm inside."

"Some people lie to throw people off-track, some do it just for fun, some don't even know they're doing it. They tell so many lies mixed with truth, they can't keep up with it themselves. What did Bethany lie to you about?"

I crossed and uncrossed my legs, peeked down at Sweet Pea to see if she needed to get out of here to go potty and give me a good excuse to scram. Big help that she is, she dozed happily at my feet.

"Bethany told me she hardly knew Whitney," I said. "Then I found out that she and Whitney were friendly rivals all through school. I know it's not much."

"Friendly rivals," he repeated.

"Yeah. Best friends one minute, then leading their own group of friends the next. I heard dribs and drabs from people. Tracy, Martha, a customer named Kristin, Rick." I drew in a big breath. "Bethany and Whitney had gone to school together from before kindergarten up through finishing school and university. I just thought you might want to know maybe she's not to be trusted."

"And you, having such a keen eye for people like Tracy, think I should take advice from you."

"Hey, you're the one asking me questions."

He doodled on the pad on the desk. "Maybe you shouldn't trust Tracy with your dog bakery." He said this like I was a child. An idiot child. "You know she wrote for that trashy magazine, *Pulse*, right?"

"She didn't do so well at it."

"She didn't do so well at a lot of things. For one thing, why would she throw a rock through the door of a store? To get dibs on the croissants?"

"Didn't Whitney have a security system? Wouldn't the fire department and police and everyone show?"

"Martha said she didn't know how to turn it on. Said she saw Tracy running off but ran in to make sure nothing was missing."

"Missing like what? A cupcake?"

"I appreciate that you have some kind of loyalty to Tracy, but have you considered the possibility that Martha isn't lying about this?" Something small shifted behind his eyes. It could have been anything. Maybe he thought Martha was lying and wanted to get my take on it. Maybe he thought Tracy had broken the window … maybe he thought *I* had.

"And sometimes a rose is just a rose. You said I seem okay? That's how I feel about Tracy." *Most of the time.*

"Don't worry, I'm looking into it. And by the way, Martha feels sorry for you. Told us people have been messing with you, coming around, calling you names. Says it's a real shame." Trumble folded his hands in front of him on the desk. "You planning on continuing to talk to people until we find who killed Whitney?"

"I sure would like this all behind me, so yes."

He considered that awhile, and I awaited his decision. If he ordered me to mind my own business, I'd have to listen. My lane was running a business and baking for dogs, not catching killers.

"All right," he said finally. "If you feel like it, go ahead and talk to people. Then we'll talk again, you and me." He leaned back in his chair and sighed. "Why isn't everyone spending their days at the beach and evenings in their mansions like the Palm Beach founders intended?"

We left Trumble's office and while Sweet Pea sniffed an interesting spot right outside the precinct door, I realized that my mind had been so much on Tracy and the rock that I forgot to mention Rick's anemic snack counter and that Whitney mentioned how she was as capable as Bethany of running her own business. Neither seemed very important, anyway. Whitney being jealous of Bethany's gallery fell in line with the friendly rivals conversation I had with Trumble, and Rick only sold a couple of fresh dog snacks. The rest were packaged and hanging from racks rather than in an enticing display case. Maybe he was a teensy bit jealous at the thought of a successful dog bakery? And it was possible he had entertained thoughts of revenge on Whitney for turning him down all those times. Didn't Martha say Whitney was getting tired of it? Scared, even? I didn't take that seriously. Whitney was probably delighted Sexy Stubble wanted to go out with her. But why did I forget to tell Detective Trumble? Could it be I was clouded by Rick's blue eyes and scrumptious scent? Maybe Rick thought killing Whitney would be a dandy way of getting back at her while getting rid of his competition, my dog bakery. For that matter, Martha could have been jealous too, though why she'd be jealous of a dog bakery when she obviously—if Sweet Pea's tepid reaction to her was any indication—didn't have an affinity for dogs. And then there was Bethany, the only one with a rich, complicated past with the woman.

Something tickled my brain. But before the tickle turned into something more concrete, a police officer marched up the steps to the precinct's front door. Sweet Pea and I dashed down to the sidewalk on South County Road. My mind turned to the fresh Blueberry Yogurt Cubes I hoped would be ready in time for the morning rush. It also turned to hopes there would *be* a morning rush.

We made our way back over to Worth Avenue. Piling out of the car on a road behind Canine Confections, Sweet Pea and I meandered to the back of Palm Beach Patisserie. A corner of thick tape stuck out from the broken window. *She better get that fixed soon if she doesn't want more problems.* Maybe Martha didn't see what she thought, or maybe she was up to something ... or maybe the police were. But what? Checking me out?

My mind was already boggled, so I shook my head, padded over with Sweet Pea to the back of Confections, and opened the door from the back patio. Sweet Pea began her inspection for errant scents and, though I needed to get to the Cubes, I slipped out the front door to get a bead on Worth Avenue. At that time of the morning, it would be quiet.

Bethany and a gentleman with movie star good looks peered into the front display of Gallery Bebe. She looked like a million bucks. Which, according to Palm Beach gossip, was approximately the amount that had been in her Trust Fund. She was a superb sight in a Lilly Pulitzer dress in the signature bold and colorful print. A pair of exotic earrings in the same colors as her dress dangled from her ears. Friend or prospective customer, the man seemed more interested in

Bethany than her art. *The girl's got the world on a string. Why would she kill Whitney?*

Before she glanced over, I headed back inside, locked the front door, and thought about what I would say to Tracy. I could fire her via text for breaking Martha's window, but how cold would that be?

I filled Sweet Pea's bowl with fresh water and set to work mixing the organic blueberries and organic plain yogurt, then scooped the mixture into ice cube trays and placed them in the freezer. I hadn't wanted to freeze them overnight because I wanted just the right consistency—not too hard, not too soft. It was a recipe I'd created and handed out in Focus Groups, and it got rave reviews from the dogs in Sun Haven.

Sun shimmered off the front window and thank goodness for that. One thing I needed that morning was something to cheer about.

Tracy rushed in the back door as I wiped up the last of the yogurt that had dripped on the counter. "I didn't do it," she blurted. "I know the police told you I threw that rock, but I swear I didn't."

"Then why would Martha say it was you?" I said from the sink as I washed yogurt off a spoon.

"I don't know. She must have made a mistake." Her eyes filled with tears. "It wasn't me! I swear!"

A customer tried the front door. We had another twenty minutes before we opened, but the heck with letting a customer get away at this stage of the game.

I locked eyes with Tracy. I needed to get the extra set of keys she had made ... then find someone to replace her ... "Want to get that?" I asked casually and turned my back to take out a tray of frozen banana slices for our first customer.

"You mean it? I can stay?"

If Trumble found something concrete, he'd bring her in, but meanwhile, something told me to go by my own instincts. I opened the small freezer door at the counter. "Your creative skills are unparalleled. If it weren't for you, this place would look as elegant and cozy as a diner with a well-worn rug."

Her eyes lit up. "Thank you!"

The schnauzer stared balefully through the glass door, so I spoke quickly. "We do have a few things to talk about, though."

"Something icky is going on," she said, scrunching up her pert little nose.

You can say *that* again.

CHAPTER NINETEEN

The following morning, I overslept, maybe from working my tail off the day before and falling into bed at midnight. Rather than a walk around the block with Sweet Pea, I jogged around the block with her to save time. As we settled into a comfortable rhythm, I gazed at the inherently elegant hedges surrounding most of the estates, none more than eight-feet tall. No, I'm not a math savant. Palm Beach is a town where measurements matter—leaf blowers require inspections to verify they emit no more than 65 decibels from 50 feet away. Locals holding a garage sale are restricted to one sign that can't be more than 4 square feet in size. Residents flying flags on their property are restricted to flagpoles that are no higher than 42 feet and flags that are a maximum of four feet by six feet … and hedges aren't allowed to be higher than eight-feet tall.

I enjoyed viewing the lush landscape while we jogged past and Sweet Pea only needed to make a couple of stops, so mostly my heart got a good workout. The furry girl's tail was wagging and her face was open and happy. All in all, life was good.

But then I rounded the block and returned to the electronic gate at the driveway. Aunt Mary's newspaper sat at her electronic buzzer, the arrangement she had made with the delivery folks way back when. It caught my eye under the street light, not only because real papers seemed to be a thing of the past, but also because of the large photo of Tracy standing in front of Canine Confections that was splashed across the first page. Since Sweet Pea's leash was in my left hand, I picked the paper up with my right and dropped my jaw at the headline: "Local Woman's Décor a Hit!"

At that early hour, the Big House was still dark. I helped myself to the paper and read with my cell phone flashlight while we waited for the gate to open. Sweet Pea couldn't care less about the article. She sniffed and snooped the Gardenias and Bird of Paradise.

I read: "Our very own Tracy Oshkosh shows keen artistic ability as lead interior designer for Worth Avenue's new dog bakery, Canine Confections. We wouldn't be surprised if it turned into the new place to be on Worth when you want to pamper your pooch. Maybe Confections will start selling warm, fresh pastry to accompany their espresso? One can hope!"

I closed the gate once we were safely inside, unleashed Sweet Pea, and trekked home to the cottage, unable to decide if I was angry or happy. Tracy got credit for making Canine Confections a success, but so what? At least it means it's being viewed as a success. After the crowd on the first day followed by a trickle of customers yesterday, I had begun to worry.

"Does Tracy know about this?" I asked Sweet Pea as we settled in to the kitchen. In the photo, Tracy wasn't looking into the camera, so maybe not. On the other hand, pigs don't actually fly. Was I that eager to fill in the blanks of my life that I'd turn my eyes every time Tracy looked to be up to no good?

Sweet Pea devoured her breakfast while I tried a few bites of yogurt. I picked up my cell and pressed Tracy's number.

"Hello?" a male voice grunted into the phone.

"Can I talk to Tracy please?"

"Hold on."

Breathless, Tracy said, "Hello?"

"It's Samantha." Not that I didn't have more pressing things to think about, but who had Tracy breathless?

"Oh, hey! I'm in the middle of working out with Benjamin."

"Back to work!" Benjamin called out in the background.

"Torturer," her muffled voice said. To me, "Everything okay?"

"You're in the paper."

"I am?"

"You mean you didn't know?"

"What paper?"

I washed Sweet Pea's dish and my coffee cup as we talked. "I don't know the name. A local one. Your picture is in it and it says your decorating skills are making Confections a hit."

"That's great!" she cried, missing my meaning.

A moment of silence passed. Then, she said in a mousy tone, "It's great, right? I mean, you wanted people to stop thinking of it as a murder site and to draw customers in."

I put away the dishes from the dishwasher. "Did you do this?"

"Do what? Get my picture in the paper? No. People have been taking pictures almost constantly the past couple days."

When I was silent, she went on. "It's good, right? More business for you?"

Who did it hurt, really?

"Yes," I agreed. "It's good."

"Anyway, all I did was toss a couple of throw pillows around and hang the pictures up … and add ceiling lights like at museums." A pause. "And arranged the snacks in the display to look like the ones at Frederika's Patisserie over in Lake Worth. And—"

"Exactly."

"Who wrote the article?" she asked.

From behind her, a voice boomed. "Now you're doing an extra hundred crunches."

"I gotta go," she said. "See you later?"

"Okay." We hung up. Because of Tracy's down-to-earth demeanor I kept forgetting she too came from money and could afford things like personal trainers.

I showered, tooth-brushed and dressed in record time, then checked in on Aunt Mary before leaving for work. She practically threw me out of her bedroom when I tried helping her out of bed.

As I drove along Ocean Boulevard, Sweet Pea stuck her head out the window and didn't bring it back into the car until we reached South County Road. As we came upon the Classic Bookshop, I slowed and tried to get a gander at the window display. A car honked behind me, so I sped up and decided to make a point of paying a special visit to my favorite bookstore in Palm Beach.

The police station was up to the left, past the fabulous fine-dining Café L Europe restaurant, and as though he were staring out his window waiting for me to pass, Trumble called my cell.

I answered the phone by way of a statement. "And here I thought suspects don't normally receive so many calls from the lead detective on a case."

"Good morning to you, too," he grumbled. "I'm calling to help you in case you're interested. I was having dinner at Renato's last night—"

"Renato's the five-star Italian restaurant on Worth?"

"Yeah. I was drinking my Sambuca and overheard the people at the table next to mine. They were talking about a new dog bakery in town, and how they heard that the owner is a murderer."

I gasped. "No."

"Yeah. I could hardly finish my crème brulée."

"Why are you telling me this?" I had only ten minutes to get to Confections in time to pop the Berry Good Dog Bites into the oven. I hoped the newspaper readers would come in droves after reading about Tracy's decorating talents.

"Because you are the one with the most to lose here." A beat of silence. Then another. "Or maybe I should say Mary is the one with the most to lose."

Like a punch in the stomach, the detective knew exactly how to get a reaction from me. "What do you want me to do?"

"I'm not asking you to do anything. But if you happen to want to visit the Goodwins and can't help giving me a call to let me know if anything interesting about Whitney comes up, I'm not going to stop you. The parents talked to us twice so far but they might loosen their tongues for you."

"Won't you get in trouble if people find out you're using me in your case?"

"Who? Little old you? You're not a suspect. You're just the new dog bakery owner in town who wants to show sympathy to the parents of the girl you found on your floor."

A pause.

"Right?" he asked.

"Okay. Right. Right." I actually did want to give Whitney's parents my sympathy and see if they were okay. Her mother was so in shock when I'd seen her the day of the murder.

I hung up with Trumble and called Tracy to tell her I needed her to hustle over to Confections. Then I hustled myself to the Goodwin mansion.

My stomach turned at the thought of seeing Whitney's parents. I put aside the horror of it because it was easier than facing it, but Whitney had been lying on the floor, right next to the display case filled with dog pastry. I reached the Goodwin's gate and pressed the intercom when a thought niggled in my head. Something about donuts and pastry. *Maybe I'm just hungry.*

Trumble had coached me on what to ask: Did Whitney have enemies? How long had she planned before opening the Patisserie? How did she come to want it in spite of all her money? Trumble told me to cozy up to the Goodwins but not make it obvious. And, he told me that his guys had miffed the Goodwins by asking too many questions, so if I sensed the slightest bit of tension, don't ruin my chances for future conversations by pushing too hard now.

Once through the gate, I drove down the winding driveway and parked in the circular lot. I asked Robert, Mr. House Manager, "Is Baron around?" before stepping inside. If the chihuahua was close, I wanted to know.

"I'll keep her in a separate wing," said Robert.

Sweet Pea nuzzled Robert's hand as he escorted us to the library we'd been in two days earlier, and then he left us to wait for the Goodwins.

A minute later, Whitney's father entered the library. "Miss Armstrong?" asked Patrick. "Little early, isn't it?"

I hadn't formally met Whitney's father before now. "Sorry."

Sweet Pea stood up to greet him. He patted her on the head in a perfunctory manner and sat in a chair opposite the couch.

"It's fine. Pamela and I haven't been able to sleep much since Whitney ..." He let the sentence trail off.

"I'm so sorry for your loss." *And surprised you're willing to see a perfect stranger in your home so soon after your daughter's death.*

"Yes. Well. Is there something I can do for you? We've had the police coming in and out asking us questions, but finally I had to tell them it was upsetting my wife too much."

"Good thing I'm not with the police." *Yup, that's me. A Liar Liar Pants-on-Fire.*

My pants were only burnt embers, however because I said, "Patrick, I'm going to be honest with you. I'm sorry about your loss, but the town—"

"Wants to run you out before you even take your shoes off?" he asked with an unamused smirk.

"Something like that. But more importantly, the sooner we find out who did this, the sooner they can be brought to justice."

"Trumble put you up to this?" He glared with an intensity that made me realize how he'd made his millions in business. Like he could see right through me.

I twisted my lips in on themselves, not wanting to spill the beans, but so bad at lying that I was afraid a squeak would pour out as soon as I tried to fib.

He nodded when I only returned his gaze. "He must be desperate."

"Only to find who …" I couldn't finish. *This man's daughter had been murdered.*

He stared at the oak floor. When he looked up, his eyes were wet. "My friends are asking me the same questions. I think they're afraid their daughters are next."

I ran through my shortened version of Trumble's Top Ten Questions to ask the Goodwins. "Whitney didn't need to open a pastry shop. She did it to prove she could make a go of it on her own, correct?"

"With a little help from her parents," he said. "There were several people who wanted that space to open a pastry shop. We did what we had to. She's our little girl." A tear slid down his cheek.

"I'm so sorry."

He straightened his back and his face hardened. "The only problem she ever had was with Bethany."

"Bethany Westwood?"

He nodded. "We're friends with her parents. We could never understand why the two couldn't be friends, to stop competing all the time. Grades, friends, boys, you name it."

Sweet Pea snuggled close. Her chin rested on the top of my foot.

"But that was a long time ago," I said. "You don't think Bethany had anything to do with Whitney's murder, do you?"

"Not at all. I was explaining to you that Whitney had no real issues with anyone."

Robert appeared with a coffee tray and scones.

Patrick asked, "Unless you'd prefer something stronger?"

It wasn't even noon, so no thank you. "This is great, thanks."

"And the dog? Sweet Pea?" His eyes misted again. "Whitney was so excited to adopt her."

Pamela Goodwin joined us fully dressed. I wondered if the pair had gone to bed these past few nights since their daughter died. "Hello, Sweet Pea," she said.

Sweet Pea, delighted to be spoken to, jumped up and whined with joy. Pamela leaned down and massaged her ears. "Whitney never got to have children, but she was so thrilled when she adopted this dog." Tears poured down her cheeks.

They seemed so raw. I had a hard time wrapping my head around why they were being so open with me, letting me into their home, opening up about their grief. But when I saw them look at Sweet Pea, I understood. They saw me as a connection, however tenuous, to their dead daughter.

Patrick twirled an unlit cigar between forefinger and middle finger, deep in thought. "It's such a shame. She worked so hard to get Patisserie open. She thought it was a lost cause and when I talked to a friend of mine to get her name moved up the list, she jumped into my arms like a little girl." He didn't break down like his wife, but I had the feeling he would as soon as I left.

Dark circles ran under their eyes like half-moons. "I heard Rick was trying to get her to go out with him," I said. "That she was scared."

"Of Rick?" Pamela said.

Patrick said, "I think she would have mentioned it to us."

Right. Because everybody knows that kids—even adult ones—tell their parents everything.

"Rick is a nice boy," Pamela said.

I smiled a little when she called him a boy.

"What about boyfriends?" I asked. "Had she upset anyone recently?"

"No," Pamela said. "She usually went along with what others wanted."

Patrick said, "To the point where if someone told her to jump, she might say 'how high' without thinking of the consequences."

Pamela smoothed her slacks. "Do you think that's true, dear?"

"How many times did we have to pick her up from parties as a teenager because somebody talked her into doing something she knew was wrong? Remember the time she and her friends broke into La Trattoria at three in the morning because they were in the mood for Italian pastries?"

"It was those friends of hers that talked her into it. She was a good girl." Pamela sniffled into a tissue.

Looking at them, Pamela twisting her tissue in her hand and Patrick straining to keep a stiff upper lip, I missed my parents and vowed to hug them harder than I ever had the next time I saw them.

"This must be difficult for you," Pamela said. "The first day of your business…"

"Don't even think about me," I said. "It doesn't compare to what you must be going through." Although now that I knew my aunt had a bigger stake in the success of my business, the pressure was on.

Sweet Pea shifted position and settled her muzzle on her front paws.

Pamela smiled at the dog. "If Whitney had a brother or a sister, maybe that would help. At least it would give us someone else to be busy thinking about. We've just been consumed since this happened."

"We haven't even had time to think about what to do about running Patisserie," Patrick said."

Pamela nodded. "Thank goodness for Martha."

Patrick marched over to Robert, who had returned to the room carrying a large, weaved picnic basket.

"Why didn't you have him throw that on the boat?" Pamela asked Patrick.

"I thought it'd be fun to carry a basket and act like the free spirits we are. Or that we used to be."

Pamela almost smiled. "I'm not sure we were ever free spirits, darling."

Lifting the basket from Robert's hands, Patrick explained, "I'm taking Pamela on the yacht for a picnic breakfast so she can stop staring at the four walls here. The fresh air will do her good."

Their house was hardly four walls. More like fifty rooms. But I got the gist and stood up to leave.

"You're welcome anytime," Patrick said, but instead of feeling good about that, I felt sad for him. He seemed so forlorn about his daughter.

They waved good-bye from their front door as I pulled onto the long driveway. They said Whitney could be talked into things, same thing I had heard from others. I moseyed my way out of the Goodwins' estate but drove to Worth Avenue at a good clip to kickstart myself into action. Who and why would someone want her in Canine Confections? Once again, the answer that sprang to mind was, it was a last-minute fight, or they had come in to somehow hurt my business.

I found a parking spot right on Worth Avenue instead of parking in the back. It gave me a great excuse to stroll past my neighbors. Even though it wasn't yet noon, the day was becoming brutally hot. I wiped sweat from my brow and glanced at the neighboring stores. Rare Books and Stamps stood on one side of Canine Confections, quiet as usual. I'd seen the owner here and there, but most of his business must have been by appointment only, because I hardly saw any foot traffic there.

Bethany's Gallery Bebe on the other side was bustling. And next to it, Martha was talking to two women, one blond, one red-haired, in front of Patisserie. Everybody looked familiar, but with so many new faces, I couldn't place them all. Martha's face looked flushed.

"I'm tired of it!" Martha shouted to her friends. The two women snickered and laid their hands on her arms as though to calm her down.

I knew how Martha felt. I was tired of things too. And snickering and trying to calm me down wouldn't help. I wanted answers.

Bethany ran out from her gallery. She and I exchanged glances. She spotted Sweet Pea and pressed her lips together.

I shook my head and left crazy-lane for the sanity of my own space at Confections.

A couple of women stood in front of Canine Confections snapping pictures. As I approached the front door, they murmured among themselves, snapped a few shots and continued down the Avenue. Through the plate glass window, Tracy's touches added an elegance and coziness beyond my ken. She was inside, smiling and petting a chihuahua, appearing so in control that for the moment, I wondered who Confections belonged to.

Bethany called from next door, "Your dogs are hurting my business."

"My dogs? I have one dog."

"The dogs that come to your dog bakery. Your customers lollygag around with their dogs. It stops prospective buyers from checking out my display window."

"I'm allowed to be here, Bethany."

She turned on her heel and disappeared inside.

"Good-bye to you too," I said aloud.

Martha, looking a little calmer than a minute ago, shook her head at Bethany and threw me an empathetic glance.

I smiled and mouthed, "Thanks." It felt good not to be alone when Miss Snootypants got rude.

Inside Confections, I made sure the owner agreed his chihuahua was okay with Sweet Pea and let her off the leash. She and the little tan wiggle-worm with the pointy nose introduced themselves by way of sniffs and wags, then settled down, Sweet Pea on her dog bed, the chihuahua at his owner's feet.

Tracy was behind the display counter, arranging the espresso machine catty corner so that it would be in the direct line of vision for anyone ordering at the display counter. *Brilliant.*

"Thanks. That's awesome," I said.

She shrugged, then grinned.

I opened the register drawer. The bills were crossed in every direction except the right ones.

"What happened?" I asked her.

Her face burned bright red.

"I had a little accident." She drew in a breath and exhaled. "The drawer dropped to the floor. I put the bills back but I forgot to fix them when I got caught up talking to the customer."

As much as I wanted to ignore Tracy's problems dealing with the money, I couldn't ignore it much longer.

Heat rose in my face until I told myself it wasn't her fault. "I put too much on you."

"I'm good with the dogs and the people. And I like how the pictures and pillows look …"

"You did great." But she had her limits. *Don't we all?*

I began to neaten up the bills in the register while Tracy swept the already spotless floor.

"You don't have to work and clean every second you're here, you know," I said. The girl seemed to bounce off the walls if she wasn't doing something.

"I like to keep busy." She tucked the broom neatly off to the side. "Oh, I forgot to tell you. Rick called. He wants you to call him back. His voice sounded kind of strange. His number is on the counter."

Tracy skipped over to schmooze with the customer and chihuahua, so I picked up Rick's number all cool-like and took it to the back. I called lickety-split but he didn't pick up, so I left a voice message. But Tracy said his voice sounded strange. And strange was one thing I didn't need any more of. My gut told me to leave Tracy one more time and head a couple doors down to Sophisticated Pet.

I returned to the front of Confections and called out to Tracy, who was busy petting the chihuahua, "Hold down the fort." Oh man, I thought, remembering the cash register. "Trace?"

She peered up from the chihuahua. "Yeah?"

"Mind coming over for a second?" I smiled at the customer.

"What's up?" she asked.

Nodding over to the register, I said quietly, "Careful with that. Money is sort of an important aspect of my business." I tried for lightness.

I made it to Rick's in less than a minute but at first glance, it appeared to be closed. None of his usual shop lights were on. I shielded my eyes from the bright day and tried to peer within. I saw no movement, but on the tile floor alongside the studded dog collars case I spotted the pet store owner's crossword puzzle book lying on the ground. Next to the book was an arm. Rick's arm.

"Oh my God," I said aloud.

I tried the doorknob. It turned easily. I opened the door a few inches. "Rick," I called, "are you okay?" Not wanting to burst in on whoever did this to Rick, I took only one step inside and reached for a light switch. Found none.

"Rick?"

No answer.

I entered cautiously moving very, very slowly with only the daylight to light my way. He was lying on the floor next to the display case. A large ceramic dog dish lay in pieces next to his head. His body was lying in a normal position, one I'd think of as a sleeping position. No blood or strange contortions. But he was out like a light. Except for his chest lifting and lowering, I'd almost think he was a goner.

I ran over and knelt beside him. "Rick? Are you okay? Talk to me."

Nothing.

I looked around, then stepped carefully around Rick's body and suddenly got the willies. If whoever did this was still here, I might get the same treatment. Much as I wanted to be a hero and make certain the store was empty of the perpetrator, I ran out the front door, looked in both directions, and when I didn't see anyone running away, steadied my eyes on Rick in case he came to. I called 911, then the Palm Beach Police Department, praying Trumble would be in. He was.

"Trumble," he said.

"Samantha Armstrong. I'm in Sophisticated Pet. Rick is on the floor waiting for an ambulance. Someone hit him over the head."

Trumble didn't miss a beat. "I'm on my way."

"Hurry, please," I urged. "I'm pretty creeped-out."

"Don't touch anything," he ordered.

Rick was inside and maybe needed help. I opened the door and went back in, careful to keep my fingerprints off everything. I knelt beside Rick again.

"Rick? Can you hear me?"

A sound came from his mouth.

"Oh, thank God! Rick?"

Nothing but a mumble came from the poor guy's lips.

"It's okay, relax," I said. "Help is on the way."

His breath was slow and steady. I inhaled a few breaths and kept my eyes peeled on both the front door and the doorway to the back room. For all I knew, somebody was still inside.

I wrapped my arms around myself and stepped back out the front door. Pedestrians moved lazily along, and some of them gave me a friendly nod the way people do in Florida. I felt a little loopy and almost announced, "Come one, come all! Another spot of violence right here on Worth Avenue!"

It seemed like forever, but probably wasn't much more than ten minutes when I heard the sound of an approaching siren. The police car pulled up with a squeal of brakes. Trumble and an officer climbed out and if I wasn't mistaken, the officer kept his hand resting on his gun butt.

We all moved inside and the EMTs got to work on Rick. He began to come to and tried to talk, but one of the EMTs told him to rest.

Trumble turned to me. "Go to Confections, Samantha," he ordered. "And don't leave it for anything. After I get done here, I'll call and you can come by the station and dictate your statement, unless you want me coming to you."

I nodded. "No thanks. That dog dish—" I offered. "It's a custom-made specialty item. They can add your dog's name in any font you want and it comes in different colors."

"Thanks for the valuable clue. You sure you're okay?"

I nodded, in a daze, and walked back to Confections. By the time I was at the front door, my shaking had almost ceased. Sweet Pea padded over to greet me, sniffed, smelled something was amiss with that amazing doggy-nose ability, and hung around at my legs.

Tracy was busy finishing the job I had started straightening up the bills in the register. She took in the expression on my face. "What's wrong?"

"Rick's been hurt."

"What?"

"The police are there now."

"I *knew* something was wrong when he called!"

"No. He couldn't have called after he was hit. He was out cold.""

Or maybe he *did* call after he was hit. I wished I didn't have to wait to find out. I retreated to the back room since we had zero customers, sat at my desk and stared at the wall. I couldn't stop reflecting on chance. If Trumble hadn't sent me to Whitney's parents, I would have come to work earlier. If I came to work earlier, I would have received Rick's call instead of getting a vague message from Tracy. And if I talked to Rick and found out what he was upset about, I might have saved him from whoever hit him over the head with a dog dish. *If, if, if. What good was all this now?*

Then Trumble called to let me know he was ready for me to come to the station and answer some more questions. How exactly was I supposed to get Canine Confections off the ground and running if I was busy finding bodies lying all over floors?

I drove over to South County Road, sat in a leather chair so large and slippery I had to balance with a straight spine, and dictated my statement into a tape recorder. I thought about asking why they hadn't gone digital by now, but I had bigger things on my mind. Like how Rick was doing, for one. And number two, who did it?

I omitted nothing. I explained my first meeting with Rick right after I found Whitney dead on Canine Confections' floor. And how Martha said Whitney had complained about him trying to get her to go out with him. And how Tracy said he called earlier that morning and his voice sounded strained.

"She that familiar with his voice?" Trumble asked.

"They all went to school together."

"'They all,' meaning—"

"Rick, Whitney, Bethany and Tracy."

He nodded like he knew this already. Which he probably did.

"Is Rick okay?" I asked. "Did he tell you who it was?"

"The doctors are making us wait until they're done giving him the once-over before we can talk to him." He reached over and grabbed a lollipop. "What else?"

"I told you everything else in my statement. I went down to his store and found him lying on the floor."

"This store is open to the public. Anybody could have gone in," Trumble said.

"I didn't touch anything except the door handle, and I didn't see anyone. But I also didn't check the place out. It's all connected, right? Whitney, Rick, me? Unless you think it's a coincidence that I keep finding people laying on floors."

The tape was taken away to be transcribed, and Trumble and I were left alone. He tore the wrapper off the lolly and popped it into his mouth.

"You sure are good at getting yourself in the middle of things," he said. "What do you think he wanted to talk to you about?"

"I have no idea. The only affiliation I see with the Whitney case is he was bugging her to go out with him. Maybe she came back from the dead and hit him over the head because she knew she could get away with it."

He offered me a droll smile. "That's probably right."

"Silliness aside, there's some kind of connection between the cases, I know that much. What are the chances there were two acts of violence within walking distance in a matter of days?"

"In Palm Beach?" Trumble asked. "Very slim."

"Right. Maybe somebody was involved who was jealous of the two getting together."

"But they weren't, right?" he asked. "According to your sources, you said she refused him?"

"You make it sound all fancy, like I have sources. Martha is the one who told me that Whitney told *her* about Rick asking her out."

Trumble scowled and shook his head. "This sounds like high school."

I had to agree.

He asked, "What makes you think Martha is telling the truth?"

"I don't know. Why would she lie?"

As usual, the detective had the gall not to answer my questions. Instead, *he* asked *me*, "What happened at the Goodwin girl's house this morning?"

"Just a couple of parents deep in grief. Oh, they confirmed Whitney could be talked into things easily, so I thought that was a good clue that someone made her come into Confections."

He nodded, studied his shoe. "Confirmed it? You heard that before?"

"Yeah. From Tracy and some others who live around here."

"Uh huh," he said distractedly. "And the rest of the folks around here? Treating you okay? The other shop owners?" He stuck the lollipop in and out of his mouth as he spoke.

"It's only been a couple of days. So far, it's okay."

"If you want, you can concentrate on getting to know the people Whitney had been hanging around," Trumble said.

"I know it's been open awhile, but why would Bethany open an art gallery? It seems like it would be a lot of work acquiring the right artists and trying to sell their art."

"You wouldn't have opened your own dog bakery if you were a Trust Fund baby?"

"Awfully deep question for this early in the morning, Detective."

I think he cracked a smile.

The stenographer came in with my typed statement: original and four photocopies. In this day and age, I couldn't believe how old-school they were. I signed them all, and Trumble gave me one of the copies for my file.

"Whose fingerprints did you find at Confections and Rick's store?" I asked. "Are they in the system?"

He regarded me with amusement. "You see that on Criminal Minds?"

"Forensic Files."

But Trumble didn't spill. I heaved a great sigh. After I left his office, I drove slowly and carefully back to Canine Confections. I wondered why I was driving like a silver-haired senior when it hit me: I could be next, and so could anybody ... Aunt Mary, Tracy, Bethany, Martha. Were *any* of us safe?

After Sweet Pea and I finished our day at Confections and arrived at the cottage later that evening, I stood at the sink and arranged a bouquet of fresh flowers I had purchased for Aunt Mary, whose friend had picked her up for an evening of Rummikub. Sweet Pea and I dashed over to the Big House to leave them for her at her front door. I settled Sweet Pea back inside the cottage, went for a quick ocean swim and returned half an hour later.

Sweet Pea and I sat in front of the cottage. I stared up at the darkening sky and tried to review the events of the day. I did all right with my mental rerun until I got the streaming sequence where Rick lay scary-still on his pet store floor. This led to Whitney's corpse and *that* was *that*. I couldn't get past it. I never thought I could shiver in South Florida, but I did. It required almost a chisel to chop up that dark scene from my brain. I did, though, by sheer will. I focused on anything positive I could think of: The sweet dog at my side. My parents and friends in Sun Haven. Aunt Mary, of course. New possible friends like Tracy, Bethany, Martha and Rick.

I wasn't going to be stupid about it, but in the decision to think of these four as friends versus foes, in that moment of needing to believe in the good, I chose *friends*.

CHAPTER TWENTY

Aunt Mary's neighbors were so far away that I hardly remembered she had any. But that evening, they must have had company over for a barbecue and game of croquet, because I smelled something delicious and heard a clanking that I hoped was croquet mallets and not cracking skulls. I fell asleep early snuggled up in my bed in the cottage with Sweet Pea at my side, but the clonk of croquet mallets had me dreaming I was in a bowling alley. Every time someone hit the pins with their bowling ball, a man behind me clobbered me over the head with a ceramic dog dish. I woke the next morning more tired than if I'd never gone to sleep.

After breakfast, I left Sweet Pea in the cottage and ran over to peek in on my aunt. She was sound asleep. I smiled at her light snore and closed her bedroom door as if I were a spy. I strolled with Sweet Pea on the beach instead of around the block, came home and gave her breakfast, and poured myself a cup of black coffee. I smiled while she ate, then sat on the couch with my coffee and looked up the hospital phone number. Once I got that, I called and asked for Rick's room. As it rang, a scary thought swirled around in my head … there was always the chance he hit himself over the head to make himself look innocent of everything going on. Brushing that aside, I went with *somebody else did it*. At least until proven otherwise.

A woman picked up the hospital room phone. "Hello?"

"May I speak with Rick, please?"

"Who's calling?" A note of concern in her voice.

"Samantha Armstrong."

Silence at the other end of the phone. Sweet Pea finished her breakfast and climbed up next to me. I stroked her and tried not to be disappointed that a woman was in Rick's hospital room, especially since I didn't know for sure he wasn't a murderer.

"Hello?" I said when the woman hadn't yet responded.

A muffled male voice said something.

"Here he is," she said.

"Samantha," Rick said in a weak but affable voice.

"How are you feeling?"

"Head hurts but I'm alright."

I massaged Sweet Pea's ears so that she tilted her head down and leaned closer for me to hit the exact right spot.

"Tracy said you wanted to talk to me yesterday," I said.

"Yeah, I did." He lowered his voice and cleared his throat, then coughed once. Softly, he said, "Mom, would you go down and get me a Crossword Puzzle book from the giftshop please?"

Mom!

A few words passed between them. He returned to the phone.

"Okay. Sorry about that," he said in a normal volume.

"Your mom is helping you? That's sweet."

"Guess I never got around to changing her as my emergency contact. Who is yours?"

"That's a little personal," I said. We were either flirting or I was playing with a hand grenade. "Why did you call me yesterday?"

"I heard something I thought you should know."

He left it at that.

"And?" I asked when he was not forthcoming.

Rick lowered his voice and spoke softly into the phone. "I don't know who's listening here. I'm stuck in this hospital bed with the door partly open and I can't get up to see if someone's outside in the hallway."

He was beginning to sound as paranoid as I had been feeling. "Let me ask you questions. You can *yes* or *no* me. Okay?"

"Yes," he said, all smart aleck-like.

"Do you know who hit you over the head?"

"Maybe."

A rustle of sheets, a shuffling noise, and the sound of a door slamming shut. Rick came back on the line.

"Okay, I can talk now," he said. "I shut the door. The nurses will probably have a fit but I've got at least a minute before they come running in. Tell me what you know."

"Tracy said you sounded funny, so when I couldn't reach you, I ran over and found you lying on the floor of your store."

"She's pretty much been running it without you, hasn't she?"

"How do you ... no. Not really. And can we get back to you please? Who hit you?"

"I don't know but I have a big bump on my head."

"So you say. Hard to see from my house."

"Where's that?"

I stayed mum. *I don't know you* that *well yet, Handsome-Who-Likes-Dogs.* And anyway, now was not the time for frivolity.

"Ignoring me, huh?" he asked. "Okay, I—"

"Why is the door closed?" a female voice shouted from Rick's end.

"Busted. Any chance you can come by?"

I jumped in the shower and half an hour later, I arrived at the hospital and found Rick's room. He was lying in bed with a bandage wrapped around his head but he looked sexy as ever.

"No mom?" I asked.

"She went to my place to pick up some supplies. The doctors said they want to keep an eye on me for a couple days before they release me."

I gestured to the chair next to his bed. "You mind?"

"Not at all. Thanks for coming."

"I didn't bring you anything."

"Were you supposed to?" he asked.

"So say the books on good manners." I pulled over a chair. "What happened to you?"

Rick said, "Somebody came from the back room of my store. They must have been hiding in there while I was with a customer. I had a little bit of a crowd earlier."

"Well, that's good," I said, my mind going to how business was doing, forgetting the priority. I cleared my throat. "Then what?"

"I got hit over the head. The police showed me the pieces of the ceramic dish. And the worst part is, it's one of my favorites."

"Who was he? Or she? Big, strong, short, tall? You got anything?"

"You sound like the police," he said. "I don't know. They came from behind." He reached up and gingerly touched his head. "They're probably going to be disappointed I lived through it."

I stared at him in horror, not that this already hadn't crossed my mind. "You think they wanted to kill you?"

Rick shrugged. "What else?"

Not that Trumble shared much with me, but how much would he want me spilling to everybody? I went with *very little*. "Why did you call me?"

"I overheard Bethany on her cell yesterday talking to somebody about a list."

"Like when I walked in on you that day in your store?"

His brow furrowed, trying to remember.

"You know," I reminded him. "When you told me your supplier didn't get the dog sweaters to you?"

"Oh, right. Right." He pressed his fingers to the bandage on his head. "This thing has everything confused in my head. Yeah, so anyway, I overheard her talking about some list and she sounded really upset. So I asked her about it. You know, I wanted to see if I was the only one having trouble with suppliers."

He rested his head back against his pillow. I gave him a moment and clamped my mouth shut before my impatience yelled at him to hurry it up.

Rick turned his head on his pillow to face me squarely. "And she got really heated! I don't know what her problem was, but she told me I shouldn't be skulking around listening to people's conversations. It was really unusual for her."

"Yeah. She's normally so even-tempered. Not snippy at all," I said.

He smiled a little. "I didn't say that. But she's not usually so angry."

"So what happened?"

"She came over to my store a little while later and apologized. But …"

He focused on the bedsheet. "I better just spit it out. She said she had been going around to shop owners on Worth who had promised they'd sign a petition to get Canine Confections off the Avenue and a lot of them changed their mind about signing it."

I sat up in my bedside chair. "What?"

"She knows people like to bring their dogs to Worth but she's saying if we start letting people come and hang out at Canine Confections, it'll lead to accidents and fights. Personally, I think she just doesn't like dogs." *Which meant Bethany was the one who Whitney had been referring to who didn't want Confections on Worth Avenue.*

"What about your store?" I asked. "She doesn't have a problem with it."

"My store is just that ... a store. Yours is more a place for people and their dogs to hang out. You have all those snacks and you sell espresso, and Martha thought maybe you'd start selling something to serve with the espresso ... it's a whole different vibe. Don't get me wrong, I'm glad you opened a dog bakery. It'll draw customers with dogs to the area, which will only help my store." He chuckled. "And really, it's all about me."

I liked his smile. But, a petition ...

"First Whitney gets killed, now this thing with Bethany. It's like everything is going crazy."

"Did you ever go out with either one of them?" I asked for completely innocent reasons having nothing to do with how good he looked even in a hospital bed.

"Bethany and I went out a few times when we were seniors in high school, but it was nothing. I think she just went out with me to make Whitney jealous. Whitney had a little crush on me back then, but like I told you, she wasn't my type." He poured himself water from the plastic pitcher.

"Tall, blond and gorgeous isn't your style?"

Rick sipped his water and locked eyes with me. "No, but medium-height, brunette and pretty is."

"Oh boy," I said, with an awkward laugh. "Does that usually work?"

He unlocked his eyes and I thought I might have embarrassed him. I hadn't meant to. He caught me off-guard.

Softly, he asked, "Why do you think I asked you to come by instead of just tell you about the petition over the phone?" He set his cup back on the bedstand. "Anyway, Whitney was sort of a party-goer. She liked to run with the crowd instead of do her own thing." Exactly how everybody explained her. "I thought maybe Bethany and I would do alright, but it never turned into anything."

"Have Whitney and Bethany been rivals even since high school? Maybe Whitney started the rumor about you asking her out to get even with Bethany?" I relaxed back into my chair, thought about that, and mumbled to myself, "Except high school was a long time ago. She couldn't hold a grudge for that long."

"You obviously don't know Whitney very well." A shadow crossed his face. "And now you never will."

"What do you mean? She did have a grudge against Bethany?"

"Ever since first grade," he said with a wry chuckle. "The teacher put Bethany center stage in the Palm Beach Twirlers Showcase."

"Baton twirling, huh?"

Rick nodded and smoothed out the sheet.

I straightened in my chair when a nurse glanced in with a disapproving look at my feet on the ledge of Rick's bed. "Bethany must have opened Gallery Bebe recently if that was the reason Whitney decided to open her own pastry shop."

"About six months."

"That's not very long. What was she doing before that?"

"Traveling and spending her daddy's money," he said with a laugh.

"And she got tired of that and opened an art gallery?"

He smiled. "Some of us like to show we don't have to rely on our Trust Fund."

Like with Tracy, I had forgotten that Rick was a silver-spoon baby. As with Tracy, his amiable manner made it easy to forget.

"You know, about that day," Rick said. A bewildered look crossed his face. "I don't know why I acted like I did."

"How's that?" I asked, truly curious.

"So … cavalier. Like Whitney getting killed wasn't a big deal. It was. It is."

We got quiet for a moment.

"Yeah," I said. "I guess it's easier to push it to the back of my mind sometimes."

"Me too."

I let that set in. "Back to Bethany. It's kind of strange she would want to open a pastry shop right next to someone she thought of as a rival."

"She and Whitney weren't really rivals. It was more like a love/hate friendship. Those of us who stayed around or came back after college are a pretty tight-knit group. Not best friends or anything, but we've known each other our whole lives." He grimaced and changed position in his hospital bed so that he could sit up a little more.

In the five or six minutes we'd talked, I learned a lot about Rick. Or what he wanted me to think. He asked me to the hospital to tell me that Bethany started a petition to get rid of my dog bakery. He, Whitney, Bethany and Tracy had grown up together and considered themselves friends to one degree or another. He, too, was wondering if whoever hit Whitney over the head was the same person who hit him. And ... he had a little crush on me. This last could be the truth, a smooth talker playing his game, or cold-blooded manipulation to get me off his trail.

Rick scratched the stubble on his cheeks with the tops of his fingers in a slow and sexy move. I needed to get a grip if I wanted to see things clearly.

I slid my chair another foot from his hospital bed. "Do you know if Whitney and Bethany got together socially?"

"You mean recently? Yeah, you know. Sometimes I'd run into them at HMF."

"What's that?"

"The swanky bar at the Breakers. Maybe I could take you for a drink after I get out of here," he said nonchalantly.

I hadn't yet decided if I could trust him. "Maybe," I answered vaguely. After a pause, I said, "All right, I'll just say it. There's a rumor that you were pestering Whitney to go out with you."

"Did Bethany say Whitney told her that? Those two … things must have been slow around here for them to come up with that one."

Why would Martha say Whitney was complaining? Or maybe the question is, why would Whitney say that to Martha? Unless I was missing something, all roads led to Whitney. Which meant it was probably Martha or Stacy.

I needed to focus, zone in on the reason I was there. "Earlier you said that whoever hit you could be related to whoever killed Whitney."

"What are the chances there'd be two violent incidents in a matter of days on our cozy little street?"

Exactly what Trumble said. "I don't know if I'd call Worth Avenue cozy, but okay … I hate to ask the obvious, but do you think Bethany could have killed Whitney?"

A sixty-ish year-old woman with a Volunteer tag knocked on Rick's open hospital door. "Hello!" She held a stuffed Teddy Bear and an envelope in her hand.

"Come in," Rick said.

The woman smiled and handed Rick the gift and envelope with Rick's hospital room number on it. "I found this on the volunteer desk in the lobby after I came back from giving directions to a visitor," she said and smiled.

"Thank you!" Rick called out as the volunteer left.

Nosy me, I leaned over for a better look at the bear while Rick opened the envelope. I flicked my finger at a tiny, loose piece of the gauze that was wrapped around the bear's head. "Is that gauze glued on by the manufacturer, you think?"

Rick's face turned ashen. "I don't think so." He showed me the card.

It said: *Next time you won't live through it.*

CHAPTER TWENTY-ONE

M y hands began to shake. Rick stared at me from his hospital bed.

"I don't know who to trust around here," he said, eyes flashing to the hallway outside his room. "We have to give this to the police."

"I'll call right now," I said and plucked my phone out from my right pants pocket.

"No. I don't want them swarming around here."

A large male nurse entered Rick's room with a cart full of bottles and needles. "What happened to that sweet mother of yours?" he asked.

Rick slid the card and bear to me. "She went to my house to pick up some things for me since you all are enjoying my presence so much."

The nurse inspected the name on one of the medicine bottles as he chatted Rick up. "Come on, now. Did she go home to get your Batman pajamas?"

"I don't wear Batman pajamas. They're Spiderman."

We exchanged glances and I left with the bear and the card, took the elevator down and searched the crowded hospital lobby for the volunteer desk. The woman who had been up to Rick's room was pointing to the elevators and giving directions to a visitor several feet away from the desk. *No wonder she didn't see who dropped the gift and card.*

Once she returned to her desk, I said, "You brought a gift and card to my friend a few minutes ago."

"Yes!" She frowned at the bear in my hand as if to ask why I was holding it. "I haven't seen that bear with the bandage in the Gift Shop."

"Do you remember seeing anyone around who may have left it on your desk?"

She smiled at the rush of people striding past. "No."

I nodded. Thought about it. "Do you know if there are video cameras here?"

"In the lobby?"

"Yes."

"I don't know. Maybe ask the security guards," she said and pointed.

I waited for the security guard to sift through a visitor's handbag.

"Did you happen to see anyone walk in with this?" He *must* have, right?

The guard seemed to have no time for funny business. He glanced at the bear and the card and said nothing. Only pointed to the line of visitors at the security gate in the entrance. Almost all were holding flowers, stuffed toys or cards. He turned away from me and back to his job. *So much for asking about the cameras.*

I left the hospital to drop the card and bear to Trumble. As I walked out of the hospital and searched the parking lot for my car, images of flying rolling pins and ceramic dishes flew across my brain. The pictures in my head didn't stop as I found my car, drove over to the police station, and stepped inside Trumble's office.

The detective took the bear and card with a grim expression. I told him what happened in the hospital. That a volunteer had brought it up, I asked about cameras, asked the security guard if he remembered seeing anyone, all for naught.

Trumble observed my frustrated face. "Alright. We'll take it from here."

"That's it? What about Rick? And the threat? First Whitney at Canine Confections, then Rick. Who's next?"

"Tell you what I'm going to do," he said.

I looked up, interested.

"I'm going to give you my private cell number. Don't use it unless you have to." He scribbled his number on a slip of paper and handed it to me.

"Why would I have to? Wouldn't I just call 911 in an emergency?"

He shook his head. "Double insurance. Just take it, alright?" he said gruffly. *Was this because I was Aunt Mary's niece?*

I checked the paper, keyed the number into my contacts list on my cell, and left. After a ten-minute drive on Ocean Boulevard, breathing salt air through the open windows in hopes of washing away the *yuck* in my head, I found Aunt Mary humming to herself as she snipped a bonsai tree. She emphatically told me that she did *"not* need anything," so I ran over to the cottage, picked up Sweet Pea, and drove toward Confections. Normally, I'd enjoy the scenic ride, but I had other things on my mind. I revised the agenda I had drawn up for my part in the investigation into who killed Whitney. The violence inflicted on Rick in his own store had shuffled my priorities, and despite the fact that I had not put much time into getting my new business up and running, I decided the murder and the assault on Rick took precedence.

I passed the Goodwins' mansion and made a mental note to prove or disprove that Bethany was in fact capable of murder … as if the answer to such things is ever so clear-cut. I also remembered to check my rearview mirror frequently to see if I could spot a tail. If somebody wanted to hurt Rick—or worse—maybe I wasn't far behind. Luckily, Aunt Mary was safe behind her fortified walls.

What would Bethany have to gain by hurting Rick? Maybe she changed her mind about him and became jealous after Martha told her he'd been hounding Whitney for a date. I had the sneaking suspicion I was missing one key piece of the puzzle. Not only an *end* piece … a super-helpful *corner*.

I arrived at Confections, got Sweet Pea settled, and began to prepare the batter for a batch of Peanut Butter Delights. Tracy showed as I was cracking a free-range egg into the bowl. Sweet Pea wagged her tail and licked Tracy's hands, then wriggled her nose at the scent of peanut butter wafting from the bowl of batter, staring at me with the intensity of one who hasn't eaten in days.

"They still have to bake," I said and rubbed the top of Sweet Pea's head. "Tracy, would you mind organizing the bags of sugar and flour in the back?"

Tracy set down her roll of paper towels. "Sure." Her smile faltered.

"You okay?" I asked while I scooped up a tablespoon of batter and slid it onto a cookie sheet.

"Yeah, why?"

"You look a little pale."

"I didn't get much sleep." A worried expression on her face didn't make me feel any better, but I didn't know her that well and didn't want to push. Though I did feel compelled to find out where she had been that morning. Dropping a teddy bear and card at the hospital volunteer desk?

I thought maybe if I shared my own concerns, it would loosen her up, get her to open, tell me something she didn't mean to. "To tell you the truth, I haven't been sleeping well, either. I don't think I'll be able to relax until they find out who killed Whitney."

"I know what you mean."

"And I hate to sound self-involved, but I'm worried about my business. Suppose it never gets off the ground?" *And suppose Aunt Mary loses Whitehall because of me?* A hot tear slipped down my cheek. I swiped it away angrily. "Sorry. I guess the lack of sleep is getting to me."

Her widened eyes made her look about twelve years old.

I tried to laugh at myself. "Tell me to give myself a good, hard slap!"

"No! It's understandable. I don't know how you're taking all these people being so mean to you."

"They're not that bad, really."

Two women opened the front door, sans dogs. "Is that where the murder happened?" one of them asked, pointing in at the floor by the display case.

"If you'll please …" I shuffled them out the front door. A man and a schnauzer in his arms followed me back inside. "Welcome to Canine Confections," I said.

Tracy disappeared into the back room. The schnauzer shivered in his owner's arms and stared nervously down at Sweet Pea panting up at her.

"Come here, girl," I said to Sweet Pea. To the owner, "Is your dog okay?"

"She's not sure what's going on yet. I just got her from the shelter."

I was happily surprised I'd run into so many people getting their dogs from the animal shelter. I had begun to think that people need to pay hundreds of dollars to feel a dog is worthy. Or that people are so particular about what kind of dog they want that they didn't even venture a look inside shelters.

"No problem," I said. "Sweet Pea, let's go to the back."

I swung open the door to the back to settle her there for the time being. Tracy, who had been leaning over a box of flour, fell sideways at our entrance. Her notepad fell out of her back pocket with large letters printed neatly across the small page: New Owner of Dog Bakery a Murderer?

CHAPTER TWENTY-TWO

"I should have known," I said.

She picked up the notepad and jumped to her feet. "It's not what you think!"

"No? Because right now I think you're using me to get a good story and get back in the good graces of *Pulse*." I thought further on that. "That is, if you ever even quit your job there. Is that what this is? You've been spying on me ever since I met you?"

"No! I promise! That's not it at all!"

I chewed my lip to keep from saying anything ugly. I needed to get back out to the front, but the last thing I wanted was to give Tracy time to come up with an alibi. "I need to get back to the customer. Mind coming with me please?"

She stashed the notepad back in her pocket and followed me.

"Is this chocolate?" the man asked at the display counter and pointed to a Carob Cluster.

"No," I said, keeping an eye on Tracy at the sink glopping soap onto her hands. "It's carob. Dogs can eat carob."

He looked down at his little mophead. "What do you think? Want to try it?"

I smiled at the man talking to his dog, forgetting for the moment the traitor washing her hands at my sink.

The little schnauzer tentatively opened her mouth and accepted the Carob Cluster. After she ate it, her nose wriggled as she searched the man's hands for another.

"Success!" I said with a grin.

"Do you have anything to go with that espresso?"

"Not yet, but I'm thinking about it."

"It'd be great if you did that. The pastry shop down the street doesn't have dog treats and the pet store in the other direction doesn't have hardly any treats for *anyone*."

"Right. Thanks."

He smiled and sat in a corner with his dog while I considered my next move with Tracy.

I leaned against the counter with my back to the customer. "I think you should leave," I said quietly to Tracy. My gut was wrenched. Well, not really. I didn't know her that well. Let's just say my gut was yanked. I suddenly missed my parents and my friends back home. Badly. *Thank God for Aunt Mary and Sweet Pea.*

Tracy dried her hands and turned to me with tears in her eyes. "It's not what you think."

"Why don't you tell me what it could be, aside from the obvious?"

She sighed and sniffled and glanced at the customer happily snapping pictures of his dog with his phone. "After I quit *Pulse*, my old boss heard I was working for you. She called and asked if I'd be interested in writing a tell-all about you and Canine Confections."

"And you said yes."

"No! I didn't!" She quickly glanced at the customer and lowered her voice. "I told them you are super nice and love dogs and serve treats that are healthy and delicious."

Why am I listening to her? Probably because I wanted to believe she was as good-natured as I had hoped. Also, I didn't want to think I was a complete idiot for entrusting her with my business like I had been doing.

She continued. "They told me they had somebody else lined up. Another writer. He was willing to write whatever they wanted. But they said that since I had already worked for them, they'd give me the first shot."

"And you took it."

"No!" Tracy said. "I told them I would do it—"

"Exactly."

"But I was just holding them off. I knew if they thought they had me in their pocket, they wouldn't give the other writer the go-ahead to do a story on you. Don't you see? I was trying to protect you!"

I crossed my arms and leveled my eyes on her. "Why didn't you tell me?"

"You've been so upset about everything going on. You just told me a few minutes ago how hard this has all been." Her eyes moved from me, down to her feet, back up to me. "I thought I would keep one more worry off your plate." She chewed her lip. "And I also wanted to save you from yourself."

"Meaning what, exactly?"

"If you ran over to the *Pulse* offices to tell them not to write an article debasing Canine Confections, that would only make for a bigger, better story in their eyes."

"And you think I would do that," I said. "Thanks."

She chewed the inside of her cheek. "Well, you went out of your way to meet Bethany, and you ran over to see why Rick called, and you went to Whitney's parent's house—"

"Detective Trumble wanted me to do that."

"That's what I mean! Why? Why would a detective ask you to question Whitney's parents?"

I returned the tray of Carob for Canines to their spot in the display case. "He said his guys weren't getting anywhere with them and asked if I'd see what they had to say."

"Right. Because he's seen how you've been since coming here. You haven't exactly been a quiet, little mouse."

"And you're saying I should be? Let people think I'm a murderer?"

"No! I'm not criticizing you. I only said that this confidence you have might have made you call *Pulse* and ruin it for yourself. You would have gone there and told them they better not do a story on you *or else*, they would have said okay just to appease you, and they would have gone to another reporter who wouldn't mind doing a big spread on the new bad seed in town that brings murder and mayhem everywhere she goes."

If this was Tracy's way of making nice with me, she was doing a very poor job.

"I just mean," she said, "that at least if *Pulse* thought I was on their side, I could squash the story. And it's been working. So far, I've been putting them off. Coming up with headline ideas for them, telling them I have a juicy story about you, and to give it time."

"And they're buying it?"

She shrugged. "They're not happy about it, but I figure the police will find out who killed Whitney soon enough and then you'll be in the clear. It'll be too late to run a story about you being the murderer."

I considered this, wanting to believe. Not having been born yesterday, I wasn't sure if I could.

"What can I do to prove it to you?" Tracy asked.

"Proof. Show me proof. Emails with dates, texts, whatever you have."

The look in her eyes told me I'd injured her. Still, she nodded. "Fine." She pulled out her cell phone and started tapping, then showed me a folder full of *Pulse* emails. I opened one and then another and another. Sure enough, they had been growing impatient and threatened to call the other writer if she couldn't come up with something about me soon.

"I don't know who to trust around here," I said quietly. "For all I know, Martha is the one behind all this. Or Bethany. Or even Rick. He could have staged the whole thing to throw everybody off that he's the one who killed Whitney." And sent himself a bandaged teddy bear and threatening card? *Come on, Samantha.*

"I'd be surprised if it was him," Tracy said. "I've known him all through school and he never came off as anything except decent."

"Which brings me to you. Why am I not thinking of *you* as the murderer?"

She tilted her head and raised her eyebrows at me like I asked her if an elephant and a giraffe could have babies. If Tracy was the murderer, that poor little Meryl Streep would topple off the podium in my mind as the greatest actress of all time.

I looked over my shoulder at the schnauzer, exhausted from his photo shoot, happily snoozing in his owner's arms.

"Have you and Rick ever gone out?" I asked.

"No," Tracy said. Her serious face checked mine, then turned playful. "Why? You interested in him?"

"That all depends if he's a murderer," I said and laughed until I realized my words. Immediately, I jumped away from the spot I'd been standing, close as it was to where Whitney's body had been lying. "I wonder if the police have narrowed their list of suspects. Whitney and whoever killed her must have come in and had a fight? I don't know."

"Unless it was planned all along. Whoever did it might have goaded her into coming here."

Which, according to anyone who knew her, wouldn't have been hard to do.

The front door of Confections flew open. The schnauzer's head peeked up from his owner's arms. Bethany threw a sideways glance at him and strode back to the display case. Wouldn't it be funny, I thought, if Bethany turned out to be the friend I hoped Tracy would be? Then, remembering Rick didn't answer me when I asked if he thought Bethany could be the murderer, I instinctively reached for the closest thing at hand in case I needed a weapon to defend myself.

"Hi, Bethany!" I said with a maniacal smile as I waved a plastic spoon at her.

She furrowed her brow at the spoon and dismissively shook her head. "Martha wants to know if you have anything for people to eat," Bethany said. "Not that I know why I'm acting as her errand girl, but there you have it."

"What are you talking about?" I asked. "This is a bakery for dogs."

"That's what I told her. Don't ask me. I'm just the messenger."

"Tell her no." *And thank you very much for trying to start a petition, by the way.* I didn't add that last statement because honestly, I had enough to worry about.

She sauntered out and flashed a frown to the dog as she swung open the door back out to Worth Avenue. The schnauzer closed his eyes and went back to sleep.

"That was strange," Tracy said.

A ray of light streamed through the clouds in my brain, not that I would share it with Tracy.

The customer gently lowered his dog to my shiny café floor. "She loved the carob treat," he said. "Think about what I said about treats for humans!" and exited.

The corner piece of the puzzle almost in place, I kept my mouth shut for now.

But I was pretty excited, and after work, I secured Sweet Pea onto her leash, and rushed to see to Gabriella, the commercial realtor who rented me the space for Confections.

CHAPTER TWENTY-THREE

I entered Luxe Realtors, a block from Canine Confections. Gabriella chatted on her phone, but waved me and Sweet Pea over. I sat down and held Sweet Pea's leash to keep her from running over and greeting Gabriella with happy kisses. She settled at my feet while we waited for the realtor to finish her call.

"What brings you here?" she said after she hung up.

"I just thought I'd stop by and say hi. See a friendly face."

She gazed at me sympathetically. "Has it been that hard?"

"Well, you know." I shrugged. "Not a lot of friendly faces, not that I can blame them."

I wanted to move this along so I had something to share with Trumble, but timing was everything. The last thing I needed was for her to see I was fishing.

"I see you got Whitney's dog."

"You know Sweet Pea?"

Sweet Pea lifted her head at her name.

"I saw Whitney walk her once or twice."

I glanced around the office with the plush carpet and rosewood desks. "Is *everything* in Palm Beach beautiful?"

She gazed at her office, then back at me. "Is there something in particular you wanted?" she asked with a courteous smile.

"I guess that's why everybody wants a business on Worth Avenue."

Gabriella straightened her shoulders with pride. "Absolutely."

"I'm just curious. If Joe Shmo from Yeehaw Junction wanted to rent out space here, would he be allowed?"

A distasteful frown crossed the realtor's face. "Where is that?"

"Yeehaw Junction is a little town near Orlando. But that's not my point. Can just anybody rent out space here?"

"Assuming they meet the necessary requirements."

I picked up a framed photo on her desk. "Cute kids." I set it down again, hoping the nonchalance was working. I lowered my voice like we were engaging in a bit of naughtiness. "But not everyone is suited, right? I mean, I got the space because my aunt helped me."

"I've known Mary for years."

"I know. Everybody seems to know each other around here."

"You slipped into your rental space easily enough," she said with a polite smile.

"But nobody was waiting on it." Giving up the nonchalance since I was so clearly not good at it, I said conspiratorially, "Sometimes there *is* a waiting list to rent a space, right?"

Gabriella gave a nod. "It's like the retail business. Either a store is empty, or ten customers walk in at once."

That's how business ran at Debbie's Bakery in Sun Haven. We expected the morning rush, but throughout the day we had either five customers at once or none.

"People flock, same as birds," I said, nodding.

"Excuse me?" Gabriella asked. She fiddled with her pen but didn't say anything more. Palm Beach residents are very polite.

Moving on, I said, "Patisserie had a waiting list, right? Whitney bumped somebody off it?"

Gabriella pursed her lips together and inadvertently glanced at the file cabinet next to her. Thank you, I said silently. She stood up and with an icy smile, asked me if there was anything more, and showed me the way out.

I skedaddled out of there with Sweet Pea and shot to my car, dialing Trumble on the way. Checking my rearview mirror to make sure I wasn't being followed, I kept a steady speed on Worth Avenue, cut over to South County Road, and parked in front of the police station.

Familiar with the protocol, Sweet Pea and I entered the station and waited while the detective met us in the foyer and led us to his office. I wondered if he owned shirts in any color except pink. At least this one was shocking pink rather than his usual pastel. "What's so important that you want me to drop what I'm doing?" he asked.

"You need to call the realtor."

"Excuse me?"

"Sorry. I'm just excited. I know you're the professional but there's a lot of talk about lists around here. I just met with the woman who rented me my space and she got very nervous when I started asking her about if there was a list to get the rental space for Patisserie. The answer is in her file cabinet, not that we need to see it. I'm pretty sure we all know who killed Whitney and why. I'm just wondering why you didn't bring them in yet."

"And you think I should keep you in the loop about our investigation?"

No need to get snippy. "I just thought you might want to know what I found out so you could, you know, speed things along, especially in light of Rick's little gift and card? Also, and I know this isn't important to anyone except me and my aunt, but I had three customers today and only one of them came in because he seemed to want a dog treat. The others wanted to know if it was the murder site."

"Gee, Miss Armstrong," Trumble said. "I'm so sorry you're being inconvenienced by a *murder*." He gave me a smirk.

I looked him squarely in the eye. "That's not fair. You know I care about getting justice for Whitney. And ... you also know that it means a lot to me since my aunt's money is invested in it."

There. *That* got his attention.

"It's only been a few days," he said. "These things take time."

"Can you at least tell me when you *might* have it wrapped up?"

"I see you have the same impatience gene as Mary." His face softened when he mentioned her name, but he stood up from behind his desk. "Alright. We're done here."

As I gathered Sweet Pea and my purse, Trumble warned, "Don't let that impatience get you hurt … or worse."

"Is that concern I hear?"

"Yeah. If something happened to you, your aunt would never forgive me."

CHAPTER TWENTY-FOUR

Monday morning, I woke up even earlier than usual. I barely got any sleep all weekend, knowing the murderer was walking free. At two-thirty a.m. I couldn't take it anymore. I climbed out of bed and went to my happy place in my cottage kitchen to try out new icings that I hoped the dogs would love. Sweet Pea was lying down with her head up, watching me with drooping lids.

"You know you can stay in bed, right?" I said to her.

She laid her head down on the floor at the front door with an abrupt *woompf*.

"I'm pretty sure we're safe all tucked in to Aunt Mary's estate. You don't have to lay by the front door." I reached down and massaged the side of her head. She leaned over for me to get the good spot, by her ear.

I gazed outside the kitchen window but with only the moon for light, could only make out the outline of the palm fronds from the tree in front of my cottage. The prospect that we *weren't* safe—even here on the Whitehall estate—had crossed my mind pretty much constantly all weekend. My hands began to shake again until I changed my focus to the measuring cup and spoons, beaters, whisk, flour, eggs, and other ingredients.

Trumble had insinuated that my impatience could get me hurt, but I didn't care. I wanted Whitney's murderer brought to justice, along with a few other things—Whitney's parents to find closure and peace, Confections to gain a foothold in Palm Beach, and Aunt Mary's estate to be securely hers for as long as she wanted it. Was that too much to ask?

After a couple of hours of measuring tablespoons and cups and pinches, my nerves had calmed enough that I was ready to move on with my day. It was still only 4:30 in the morning, so I cooked up a few sweet potatoes to play with in new recipes. A few hours later, after several failures but one shiny new recipe involving the sweet potatoes and honey, I checked on my aunt. Then I showered, fed Sweet Pea breakfast, poured a piping hot cup of coffee with extra cream and sugar for comfort, and drove to Worth Avenue. I parked in front of Canine Confections, clicked Sweet Pea's leash to her collar and led us to the front door, not ten feet away. Outside, the sky had the color and weight of a wet, grey down comforter. Not a wisp of air was moving, and even the palm tree's fronds on the sidewalk in front of Confections looked despondent. It was a crushing atmosphere, as if a storm was skulking nearby and might leap at any moment.

I completed my morning set-up earlier than usual. Tracy straggled in a minute later, sleepy-eyed. Sweet Pea greeted her with her usual wagging tail and lolling tongue.

"Hi, Sweet Pea," Tracy said, but she didn't seem to have the energy to lift her hand and pat my pup's head.

"Everything okay?" I asked.

"Next time your friends tell you girls' night will have you home by midnight, don't believe them."

I wanted to feel light and chipper and happy, but it wasn't coming. With an insincere laugh in the name of politeness, I said, "I'm sure you could have gone home any time you wanted."

"Where's the fun in that?" she asked with a sleepy chuckle and began rearranging the Tail Waggin' Treats I spent twenty minutes on.

"You really are so good at that," I marveled. "Why do I even bother trying?"

"But if I tried baking a snack on my own, none of the dogs would eat it."

"You'd be surprised how undiscerning dogs are," I said and rubbed Sweet Pea along the top of her back. She responded with a lick.

"How do you feel about different levels in the display case? The eyes like having different levels to look at." She bent her knees slightly and looked at the case, then stood tall and looked again.

"Go for it," I said.

I left Tracy in her zone fixing the display trays in the case, then moseyed over to the café to pick up a stray napkin that had somehow gotten beyond her notice. Outside the plate glass window, Aunt Mary's assistant Alice strode past. I almost never see her, so I threw open Confections' door and called out, "Alice!"

She turned, paused. Her face drew up in recognition. "Oh, hi."

We met up midway on the sidewalk, almost in front of Bethany's gallery.

"I forgot your dog bakery is here," she said. Her face looked a little worn.

"You didn't happen to go out on girls' night last night, did you?" I joked.

Alice looked up at me, confused. "No."

"Everything okay?"

"Yeah. I'm just up early doing a little shopping."

"For my aunt?"

Alice's answer threw me for a loop. "No."

Friendly as ever.

She said, "Tell your aunt I'll miss her."

"Where are you going?"

Bethany exited Gallery Bebe and inspected her display window. She glanced over, then turned her back to us.

"I'm not going anywhere. It's your aunt."

Was Aunt Mary keeping something from me? Was something wrong with her health?

"Didn't she tell you?" Alice asked.

"Tell me what?"

Martha strode out of Patisserie, all smiles and strong arms. "Hey, Bethany!" she shouted as she wound her way through customers on her pastry shop patio. My dog bakery, on the other hand, was completely devoid of people except for Tracy.

"Hello, Samantha," Martha called out as she strode over.

No offense, Martha, I wanted to say. *But I don't have time for niceties just now.*

"Hello," I said when she joined us.

Alice nodded.

Martha laughed, I guess at our frowns. "Everything okay?"

After I assured her we were fine, she said, "That's good. Can't be too sure around here. You never know who you can trust. You heard about Bethany's list, right?" She glanced at the art gallery owner, threw me a smile, and strode back over to Patisserie.

I turned back to Alice. "What's wrong with my aunt?"

From the pained expression on Alice's face, I thought the worst. "She said she can't afford me anymore." Which meant Aunt Mary's finance guy must have called her and told her things were even worse than he thought.

Grateful my aunt's health wasn't at stake but upset at the turn of events, I said, "I'm sorry. I'm sure she'll have you back as soon as things take an upswing."

She nodded. "Whatever. Meanwhile, I'm hitting the pavement for something to wear for interviews."

On Worth Avenue? I wanted to ask. *How much do personal assistants in Palm Beach earn?*

Alice and I said good-bye and as I watched her peek into the Chanel window, I thought maybe I might have a little chat with Aunt Mary about how much she had been paying her assistant. Not that I was in a position to give anyone advice about money. I just didn't want her generosity—with me, or anyone—to put her in the poorhouse.

After Alice took off down the sidewalk, I lifted my phone out of its typical spot in my front right pocket to call my aunt. But she would only tell me everything was fine. I would deal with that later. Meanwhile, I went about my plan to move things along by stirring the pot … get people talking, watch them more closely, maybe even get emotions to rise. I just wanted this murder investigation done. Not a brilliant plan maybe, but at least I could call it my own. And feel like I was doing something besides waiting.

I swung open Confections' door. "Let's saddle up," I said to Sweet Pea. We drifted past Rare Books and Stamps and over to Sophisticated Pet. Through the plate glass window, I was happy to see Rick out of the hospital and chatting with a customer. My next thought, *I'm so glad everybody has customers but me,* made me feel as selfish as I was. "I do not like myself very much right now," I said to Sweet Pea. She lolled her tongue up at me in a smile. "Yeah, thanks—and no offense, but you'd like me even if I showered only once a month."

Rick spotted us and waved us in. I swung open the shop door, smiled at a rack of $150 dog sweaters, and waited while he finished with a customer. After Rick finished explaining how the special blanket in his hands could reduce anxiety, the customer decided on the blue plaid, paid, and left.

Sexy Stubble didn't have so much as a bandage on his head. "Florida thunderstorms are no friend to dogs," he explained. "They get scared out of their wits."

I loosened the lead on Sweet Pea's leash. She ran over and licked his hand.

"I know you said she's this friendly to everyone, but you can't tell me she's this loveable to them." He squinted his eyes at me. "What's up?"

"I'm glad you're feeling better." He looked pretty good considering a few days ago he was lying in a hospital bed. "I've decided to have a little gathering tonight for my neighbors at my shop."

"Even the stamp guy?"

I smiled. "If he was ever at his shop, then yes. I'm sure I would invite him."

"What's this about?"

"Ever since you got that teddy bear and card, I've been a little freaked out."

"Yeah, no kidding." He swiped a hand across his mouth.

"And even before that, it's been so awkward around here. I thought we could all make a fresh start with each other."

"And you came in person to ask. Classy."

I smiled and waited for his answer.

"Could I bring anything?" He waved a bag of All-Natural Beef Chips.

"No, thanks. I have it covered," I said and left.

Next, I went to Martha's Patisserie and waited for her to finish boxing up éclairs for a customer. As per usual, I had to hold Sweet Pea back from trying to lick the customer with the generosity Santa Claus gives his favorite child.

"What are you doing over this way?" asked Martha.

"I'm having a little get-together tonight at Confections for my closest neighbors."

"Alright, but I don't think you'll get the stamp guy to come."

She rounded from behind the display case. Sweet Pea tugged her leash over to the case.

I laughed. "I love cannolis too, Sweet Pea."

"It's cannoli," Martha explained. "Or cannolo if you're talking about only one. Anyway, what's this about a get-together?"

"All the usual suspects will be there. You, me, Tracy, Bethany, Rick."

"Sounds good. Want me to bring anything?"

"I've got it, thanks."

Sweet Pea pressed her nose to the glass of the display. I pulled her back gently.

"Sorry," I said. "I'm not used to having a dog yet. Want me to Windex that?"

"Nah. I'll do it after you leave."

Sweet Pea and I moved on to Gallery Bebe to invite Bethany. After she agreed to come—surprising me that everybody was available on such short notice, we sat in the front of her gallery like she and Martha had done a few days prior.

Bethany crossed her legs elegantly and regarded the artwork in her front window. "People think that because I have money, this gallery doesn't mean anything to me, but they're wrong."

We're sharing now?

"Everybody thinks people like me feel entitled."

"I don't think everybody thinks that way."

She chuckled lightly. "Well, then, we're not talking to the same people. Anyone I know who doesn't come from money tells me how the privileged few receive favors most people would never dream of."

True, I thought. America may be the land of opportunity, but success sure comes easier to those born with a boatload of money and connections.

"No offense," I said with a laugh, "but how many people do you talk to outside of your circle?"

"Touché," she said. Even her *customers* weren't the type of people who shopped in the *PennySaver*.

Sweet Pea tried to rub against Bethany's leg again.

"Pretty sure she doesn't want to pet you, Sweet Pea."

I opened my mouth to address the petition but for some reason, Bethany couldn't seem to stop chatting. "What people may not realize is we're just people. Me, Whitney, Rick, Tracy ... we've known each other all our lives. Losing Whitney is a big loss for us. When it came down to it, Whitney and I were very good friends."

Maybe, maybe not. *I'll find out soon.*

CHAPTER TWENTY-FIVE

Monday evening, everything was in place for a friendly little gathering. If something substantial came of it, that would be icing. At the very least, it would give me more information than I'd gotten so far from various detectives, reporters, shopkeepers, parents, commercial real estate saleswomen and aunts.

Tracy ran home to get changed, so at seven p.m. sharp, Sweet Pea and I were the only ones there to greet Rick, the first to arrive. He looked good as ever in his straight-leg jeans and linen shirt opened at the collar, and he held a red ball in his hand that he laid in Sweet Pea's mouth.

"Thank you!" I said.

Sweet Pea wagged her tail, dropped the ball at his feet, and lifted her chin to him in an invitation to *throw it please*.

He threw it a couple of feet. She slid on the glossy floor.

"Be careful!" I said to her. To him, I said, "How's your head? All better?"

He knocked his knuckles on top of his head. "All my marbles still intact."

I laughed. "Dork."

"Got a problem with that?" he said, and this time I was pretty sure he was flirting.

Next came Martha and Bethany. Sweet Pea started to pad over, but then Rick tossed the ball and she darted after it.

"Bethany, that green blouse brings out your eyes. Gorgeous," I said.

"Thanks, luv."

Huh. I was *luv* now.

Tracy showed soon after. We settled everybody at the tables with drinks and snacks. She looked adorable in a solid bright red shift dress. I returned to the small area behind the display case and observed the four people I'd gotten to know in the past week. One of them was a murderer, and I was pretty sure I knew which one.

Tracy ran over. "Need help?"

"No, thanks. Just enjoy yourself." It was important no one was in on who I thought the murderer might be. They would never stay or if they did, they would act wonky. Wonky, I didn't need.

Tracy raced back over to Rick and Sweet Pea. She and Rick played fetch with my girl. Martha joined me behind the display case and maneuvered the phyllo dough for my mini-baklavas like a pro.

"I haven't worked with phyllo dough that much," I said. "Whenever I tried, it falls apart in my hands."

Amy Hueston | 239

Martha smiled. "Once you work with it enough, your fingers get muscle memory."

"Well, that's something to look forward to," I said, sighing when a layer of it crumbled between my fingers. Frustrated, I asked, "How did you learn how to bake?"

"Pastry School. My parents scraped up half and I worked nights to pay the rest."

"Nice parents."

Martha reached over for my phyllo dough and somehow miraculously made a tiny cup with it.

While Martha worked her magic with the dough, I peeked over at Bethany in the café. She turned to her glass of champagne when I made eye contact.

"Bethany's being awfully quiet," I said.

"Whitney's funeral was Saturday. Maybe she's upset about it." Martha made a face.

"What?" I asked.

"Oh, nothing. It's just, if you saw how those two sniped at each other, you would think her sadness over Whitney's death was a little … insincere."

I left Martha to finish up the baklavas, opened another bottle of champagne, and served everybody a glass while classical music played overhead. Beethoven, then Bach. I loved it, plus I thought it would be soothing, something our little strip of Worth Avenue needed.

Sweet Pea kissed almost everybody, and though her lack of affection was no proof, it at least served as an arrow. Trumble I assumed, almost had his own proof, not that he filled me in on anything, the louse. I smiled at the thought of him and couldn't wait to get the goods on him and Aunt Mary once this all settled down.

After about half an hour when everybody was a little more loosey-goosey, I began to shake things up, if nothing else, to get some energy going and answers made about who might have killed Whitney. The heck with Trumble's warning. Enough was enough.

I sat at Bethany's table and took a sip of champagne. "I heard Whitney opened her pastry shop to prove she can run a business too, like you."

"Where did you hear that?" she asked.

"Do you think that's true?"

She shrugged with one graceful shoulder. "She was always competing with me."

I gauged my words. "I heard it went both ways."

She looked at me like she wanted to wring my neck, which was precisely the mood I was going for. Enough with the Palm Beach niceties. We needed someone to spit out the cold hard truth and move past this.

Bethany said, "Remember Martha told you Whitney's parents bypassed all the other people to get dibs on Patisserie? Did she ever tell you that *she* was first in line for it?"

"Where did you hear that?" Martha asked.

"Gabby and I went to school together," she said.

"She's lying," Martha said. "Watch out for her."

Ignoring Martha, I asked Bethany, "The leasing agent?" I asked. "Did you tell Detective Trumble that?"

She threw me a withering look.

And since Trumble so rudely kept me out of his loop, I had no idea and thought I was giving him a big revelation from Gabriella's file cabinet.

I turned to Martha. "Is that true, Martha? Were you on a list?"

Rick stood up and spread his arms in a *let's all be friends* gesture. "Alright, come on, everybody," he said. "Accusing each other isn't going to help anything."

Martha set a tray of my mini quiches onto a table. "Oh, I think it will help a lot if we all clear the air. Tracy, why don't you tell Samantha how you threw a rock into Patisserie?"

Tracy's eyes filled with tears. "But I didn't!"

I had been warned about not letting everybody muddy the waters and how some people lie to do just that. They'll tell lies big and small to accomplish this, matter of fact.

Bethany said to Rick, "I know why *you* want us to let this all go. Why don't you tell us what you were doing roaming around Samantha's dog bakery the morning Whitney was found?"

"I'm not allowed to walk around the neighborhood?" asked Rick. "And I suppose I hit *myself* over the head in my store?"

"To make yourself look innocent?" Bethany asked. "Maybe."

Rick looked around at all of us. "And who had the hospital volunteer bring up a teddy bear and threatening note?"

"What?" Martha asked.

"What are you talking about?" asked Tracy, horror in her eyes.

"Tell you the truth, Bethany," Rick said, "I thought there was a chance it was you who hit me."

"Why would I do that?" Bethany asked.

Rick shrugged.

Martha spouted out, "Because you were jealous of him asking Whitney out so much."

"I didn't ask Whitney out," Rick said. He turned to Bethany. "And I never believed you were the one who hit me. But I don't know, you and Whitney were always sniping at each other. I thought you finally had it out in the form of a physical fight."

"Thanks," Bethany said.

"It was just a theory …"

Everybody began talking and accusing each other at once. The cacophony was reaching a high and I prayed clarity would come. I sat back in my café chair with my glass of champagne and watched everyone as things were brought to a head.

Ten minutes later, everybody seemed to have worn themselves out. They sat in their chairs in my café with sullen looks, sipping or guzzling from their glasses.

I said quietly and as politely as I could, "I don't mean to get us all riled up again but actually, Rick, I thought maybe you murdered

Whitney. You're the only one who might think of me as a competitor and there was a rumor you had been asking her out again and again lately." We locked eyes.

Bethany chuckled.

"What?" I asked.

"I never believed that for a minute." She turned to Martha. "Sorry, Martha. I know you thought you and Whitney had this whole friendship thing going, but if you knew her better you would know she tended to talk herself up sometimes."

Martha looked hurt, then angry. "I shouldn't be surprised," she said with a shrug. "Just because I'm not from around here—"

"I'm not from around here either, Martha," I said.

"May as well be. You got that aunt."

Tracy was sitting quietly observing everyone. Her eyes were round as my espresso cups. "You're awfully quiet over there, Tracy," I said.

She peeked at Martha, maybe still stung by being yelled at for breaking her window. She really did seem like such an innocent. She would be the last one everybody would picture as the killer in a movie and I once again thought how that probably confirmed she was the murderer.

Bethany, a little drunk, said, "Maybe someone is trying to knock us all off. Kill all the shop owners on our strip of Worth Avenue and have their own little shopping piazza."

"It's not a piazza unless it's square," Rick said.

"Did they teach you that at your fancy school?" Martha asked, smiling at Rick.

I drank a few sips from my glass and petted the pooch at my feet. "Maybe not kill us, but I do think someone wanted to run me out of town by leaving Whitney's body on my floor."

Tracy said, "You don't think it was an accident?"

Bethany said, "What kind of accident? The rolling pin flew by itself and landed on Whitney's head?"

Tracy leaned back in her chair, shot down again.

"Why is everyone so rude to Tracy?" I asked. "Geez."

She looked at me with a grateful smile.

Rick, tapped in to solving the puzzle, wasn't deterred. "Knowing Whitney, she was talked into coming in that morning."

"Why would someone do that?" Tracy asked quietly.

"So they could kill her, Einstein," Bethany said.

"Bethany! Enough!" I said.

"And ruin Canine Confections' reputation before it had a chance," Rick said as though he hadn't been interrupted.

Martha asked, "What makes you think somebody talked her into coming in?"

"Because we all know how she was all through school," Bethany offered, and swilled the last of her champagne.

Rick nodded. "Anyone who knew her knows all you had to do to get Whitney to follow along was make a suggestion."

Sweet Pea curled up at my feet.

"Let's resolve this. Who had motive?" I asked, meaning business.

Bethany snickered. "Seriously? Who are you now, Judge Judy?"

"Is that why you called us here?" Tracy asked me, hurt in her eyes.

I looked from one to the next of my four guests, then down at Sweet Pea. "I just wanted to clear the air," I said softly. "I thought you all might be as tired as I am of tip-toeing around each other. I thought maybe it would help."

"The police are probably ready to wrap up the case any day. Pretty sure they don't need us," said Bethany.

"I'm pretty sure you're right," I answered.

Bethany tilted a champagne bottle into her glass but only a drop came out.

"I have more in the back refrigerator," I said and grabbed the empty champagne bottles.

I glanced over my shoulder before exiting to the back room. My guests looked a little tipsy and a lot peeved. I let my impatience get in the way of the natural course of action, whereby Trumble would finish his investigation without my help. Or, as he probably would call it, interference. Everybody had been moseying along, not thinking they were suspects. Now they were all on red-alert. And here I made fun of Aunt Mary for her impatience with her knee.

I entered my back office, shutting the door between front and back, and opened the back door to the patio. The fresh—well, humid—evening air felt good as I dropped the champagne bottles into the recycle bin and scooted back inside. I swung open the walk-in refrigerator, reached for a bottle of champagne, and bolted out of the way of a large cardboard box of butter cartons falling off the shelf.

Rick peeked into the back room. "Samantha?"

I ducked my head out of the walk-in.

"We're all going to head out," he said. "I just wanted you to know."

"I guess I made bad blood between everybody now, huh?" I said, half-closing the walk-in door so he wouldn't see what a klutz I was. I grabbed onto the doorframe and stayed still to avoid tripping over the cartons of butter at my feet.

He shook his head. "Nah. I get it. I was getting tired of the shifty glances between all of us, too." He smiled his movie star smile. "Thanks for tonight and see you soon," he said and left.

Hands on my hips, I looked down at the cartons scattered on the walk-in floor and knew I had to deal with them or risk breaking my neck next time I dashed in for a carton of whipping cream.

I began to pick up the cartons, until it hit me that Sweet Pea was still in the café and everybody had left. Leaving the mess in the walk-in, I opened the door between front and back of Confections and checked that she hadn't slipped out the door while they exited for a walk on her own. She was sleeping peacefully at the front door. I slowly stepped over her, locked it, then returned to the back room. I opened the walk-in and sighed at the butter cartons sprawled across the floor. A few of them had somehow flown even *behind* the walk-in door. I almost completely shut it to get at them and wrapped an arm around myself to ward off the cold. As I squatted to retrieve them, I thought

I heard movement somewhere in the back office, and saw a flash of peach through the crack in the slightly open walk-in door. Someone was in the back with me and it wasn't Tracy ... there wasn't a speck of peach on that red dress of hers. I bit down on my lip to keep from screaming.

My cell phone was in my right pocket. I didn't know how fast 911 would come so I decided I'd call Trumble's cell too in case he'd speed here first. With fingers that almost seemed boneless, I lifted my cell out of my pocket, taking great care not to make any noise. Thank God I kept the settings to all sounds *off*. I pressed 911 and when the operator picked up, I whispered my address and that I needed help. Next I pressed Trumble in my Contacts List.

"You didn't waste any time calling this number," Mr. Sunny said into my ear. "Everything okay?"

"Detective," I breathed. "I'm trapped alone with someone in the back room of Canine Confections."

"I'm close. I'll be there in three minutes," he said, not wasting a second. "Stay quiet. Hide."

"Where? Behind the cartons of creamed cheese?"

I hung up my cell and slid it back into my pocket so slowly ... so carefully ... my trembling hands would probably drop it to the hard floor with a loud crash.

I had been pressing my luck. It was why I invited them all here. To get things moving, shake things up. They were moving, alright. And somebody didn't appreciate it.

My legs were shaking. I had two options on hiding. Stay in the refrigerated walk-in or go out into the back room and greet whoever was there. The intruder was only a few feet away, right outside the walk-in door.

How had they gotten in? I locked the front door. I wrapped both arms around myself for warmth while I was thinking ... I quickly retraced my steps ... I left my guests for more champagne, but first I threw out the old bottles in the recycle bin. On the patio.

I left the back door open.

CHAPTER TWENTY-SIX

The only place to hide was right here in the walk-in. Goosebumps ran up and down my arms. I could survive the refrigerator temperature until Trumble showed. Surviving whoever was out in my back office was another matter. I opened the walk-in door an inch with the tiniest of squeaks ... and peeked out as the light in the back office went out. I couldn't risk leaving the momentary safety of the refrigerator in the hopes they left. I also couldn't stay in here too long and risk Sweet Pea getting hurt. At this last thought I panicked.

Mouth dry, stomach lurching, I bolted out the walk-in and crashed into someone. They paused, startled from my abrupt entrance maybe, and I hurled myself on top of them. I wrapped my left arm around a thick neck, and with my right hand grabbed a handful of hair and pulled, hard as I could, thanks to hours of watching female superheroes on television. My next instinct was to scream but the last thing I needed was Sweet Pea hurting herself trying to bite through the door between café and back office and get hurt. Or for whoever *this* was to hurt her.

Something hard knocked me under the chin. I grunted and howled, but grabbed an arm and squeezed the neck. A hard clinking sounded on the floor, something like a baseball bat.

"Let go," gasped a thin voice. Nails began piercing the flesh in my forearm. I loosened my grip around the neck when sharp nails dug in and slashed my arm. I swallowed a scream to keep Sweet Pea from hearing me, but it was too late ... here she was ... her fur on end so that she appeared ten times her size ... a low growl coming from her mouth ...

"Sweet Pea, no -ooooo ...!" This dog was *not* going to get hurt.

The light in the back office came on. My attacker spun to face the person who'd turned it on, shoving me off and into the handle of the walk-in for one last stab of pain when my forehead met steel and I slumped to the ground.

Trumble stood at the door between front and back rooms pointing a gun at Martha. A rolling pin lay at her feet. And Trumble looked at me like he wanted to kill me. "You know there's a difference between *helping* and *interfering*, right?"

"Sorry," I murmured.

Gesturing toward the rolling pin with his gun, Trumble said to Martha, "Yours this time?"

Sweet Pea ran over to me sitting on the floor at the walk-in and wouldn't stop licking my face. "I'm okay, Sweet Pea. It's okay!" Though my arms and shoulders felt like a marching band ran over me, I reached my hands up to hold her little face in front of mine and gaze into her eyes as proof. "See? I'm good." To Trumble: "How did you get here so fast?"

"Something told me to keep an eye on you. I was down the block."

Aunt Mary.

"Some*thing* or some*one*?"

He shot me a look.

"Either way, thanks."

Sweet Pea chuffed, sat with her back to me facing Trumble and Martha, and waited.

Where were the rest of the police?

Martha fell to her knees, an inch from the rolling pin. She took in my scratches and bruises and the rolling pin at her side, and turned to Trumble. "Samantha was going to kill me like she killed Whitney."

"Save it," Trumble said.

Martha changed tangents. "You have no idea what Whitney did. She took Patisserie right out from under me!"

"Put your hands against the wall," Trumble said firmly.

She grabbed the rolling pin and held it high above her head. Sweet Pea let out one piercing bark.

"My gun will do more damage than your rolling pin," Trumble promised. "Set it down and put your hands in the air. Next time I ask, I won't be so nice."

Martha did as she was told.

This back office was too tight. I didn't like Sweet Pea being between me and Martha. My loyal protector complained with a whine but I wrapped my arms around her and moved her behind me to keep her from Martha's reach.

Trumble held the gun point blank at Martha while he took out his handcuffs.

"You weren't really hanging around watching my dog bakery, were you?" I asked.

Trumble didn't take his eyes off Martha for a moment, but he did shake his head and scowl, I suspect, at my questions. "Can this wait?" he said through clenched teeth.

Another officer was sure to come along soon, but I could see from Trumble's expression that he wanted to cuff Martha as soon as possible, especially since she appeared one card short of a full deck.

Martha must have read his expression too, because she dove for the rolling pin again. Trumble jumped on her back before she got to it.

She cried, "You need to hear my side—"

Trumble snapped the cuffs on her before the sentence was out of her mouth. "I don't need to hear anything." He holstered his gun.

Martha stood with her hands cuffed behind her back but she wouldn't shut up. "Before you opened," she said to me, "I heard you were going to serve espresso. It was only a matter of time before you added pastries for people. Do you think I was going to let that happen?"

I gingerly felt what had to be a bruise on my forehead. "And that's why you killed Whitney and wanted my name smeared? To get rid of her and run me out of town?"

She shrugged. "Two birds, one stone. And Rick would make three." She beamed. "Imagine, I could sell pastry for people *and* their pets, and then expand into pet products like Rick has."

"How do you figure?" I asked. "I was still alive."

"One way or another, I'd get rid of you," she said. She couldn't seem to help herself.

Martha breathed in and out with a heavy sigh. "*God*, it feels good to get this off my chest."

I tried to stand up, but my legs were still shaky. Sweet Pea stood up as I moved and, watching my every move, panted at me as I sat back down on the floor. Trumble held his hand to his holstered gun while he kept his eyes on Martha and radioed it in.

"Did you spray-paint the graffiti on my window?" I asked Martha.

Her chest rose and fell in deep breaths and sweat glistened from her face. "I got friends in high places."

"The redhead," I said, nodding.

She snickered. "My neighbor in West Palm."

Trumble's voice rose above ours for a moment. "She's cuffed and ready to go."

Martha winced.

From the floor, I asked her, "How did you get Whitney to come in here that morning?"

"What everybody said. She'll follow anyone. I told her I heard somebody scream and that there was no time to call the police, then clunked her over the head with a rolling pin."

"And throwing suspicion on Bethany? Making sure I knew she and Whitney had been rivals? Telling her Rick was dying to go out with Whitney?"

Martha chuckled, then grimaced at Trumble when he stepped closer. "He didn't want to go out with Whitney. From what I could see, he has his eye on you."

Rather than act as giddy as I felt from that little revelation, I remembered the current situation and looked up at Trumble. "All this time she was just throwing lies around to make things so murky that no one knew *what* was going on."

"Oh ye of little faith," he said. "I told you to be patient." He shook his head at me again. "What made you think having everybody over was a good idea?"

Thankfully, I didn't have to answer. The back door to the patio swung open. Sweet Pea barked once and before I knew it, my back office was filled with officers and EMTs.

The EMTs helped me to my feet and checked me and Martha out, somehow managing to check Miss Patisserie even with her handcuffs on. They told her to raise her arms and I spotted a brooch with a large M in a fold of her peach top.

"Where did you get that?"

"None of your business, that's where."

After they were done, Trumble sat her in my desk chair while he met with one of his people. With nowhere to go except out of the room, I found myself standing next to Martha, making sure to keep Sweet Pea on my opposite side.

"She never forgave me," Martha said with a gesture of her chin to Sweet Pea.

I gazed down at the girl. "No, I suppose she didn't."

"The police have been onto me ever since the phony call about Tracy breaking my window. I guess I was pressing my luck." Her voice sounded defeated.

I knew my instincts were on the money with Tracy. I sighed and looked at Martha. "Why did you do it? Go to such lengths that you actually killed somebody?"

"You work your whole life. You win baking competitions in elementary school. Your parents work extra jobs so you could take extra classes in advanced cake decorating. Then one day, you graduate pastry school, your parents sell their house, and you find a perfect location for your pastry shop."

"Your parents sold their house?" That was above and beyond to me, until I remembered Aunt Mary was in danger of losing her estate for the same reason.

"They're living in a rental house in West Palm now. I was top of the list to buy Patisserie from the previous owner. Then out of the blue, I got a call that someone squeezed in ahead of me. Just like that." Tears slid down her round cheeks.

I felt for her, I did. But then I thought about Whitney's parents, home right now, grieving for their daughter. "Your parents can come visit you in jail, Martha. Whitney's can never see her again."

Her face crumpled. "I guess I let my emotions get the best of me."

"Ya think?"

"If they put me in jail, promise me something?"

"I'm not promising you anything. But just out of curiosity, what is it?"

"Maybe bring me some cannoli every once in a while?"

CHAPTER TWENTY-SEVEN

Detective Trumble and his staff finished up within an hour. With Martha carted off to jail and everyone else gone, he popped a chocolate Tootsie Pop into his mouth and strode out the front door. I had to smother an impulse to grab his sleeve and tell him to wait for me to lock up. I felt so vulnerable. I supposed that one day I would get used to the idea that nobody was trying to get rid of me or my dog bakery anymore.

First, I locked the front door, then I double-checked that the back door was locked too, and finally I sat in the café to catch my breath.

I had just made it. If Trumble had been any later, who knew what would have happened? I shook all over. Sweet Pea didn't leave my side, and that only made me feel guilty for worrying her. I tried to keep my emotions in but it all came out at once. I put my head in my hands and cried. After a minute, the sobs turned into whimpers, then sniffles.

"I'm fine," I said to Sweet Pea and gave her a bright smile to convince her.

My body felt limp. I cleaned my face with one of my fancy napkins and brewed a shot of espresso so I could feel the comforting little cup in my hand. Then I sat in the café and drank it while Sweet Pea and I gazed out at the twinkle lights at the shops across Worth Avenue. My muscles ached, and the bandage on my forehead probably made me look like Frankenstein but all in all, I was okay. And so, thank God, was Sweet Pea.

Twenty minutes later, I washed out my cup, clipped the leash onto Sweet Pea's collar and switched off the light at the front door. As soon as I opened the door to leave, I ran face to face with my aunt.

"Aunt Mary, what are you doing here?"

"I've been calling you for the past half hour. I couldn't wait. I needed to see if you were okay."

"Impatient much?" I teased and flicked on the overhead lights.

"What happened to you?" She leaned on her cane with her right hand and gently laid her hand to the bandage on my forehead with her left.

"Nothing. I'm fine."

"Nothing?" Her tone meant all business. So did her hardened frown.

"We found out who killed Whitney."

She leaned on her cane. I shut the front door and locked it. "Come in and have a seat. I'll get you some water."

She followed me to a café table and sat down. "Who was it?"

"Martha Crenshaw."

"Whitney's assistant who planned on taking over Whitney's pastry shop?"

"Yeah, well, apparently it was supposed to be her pastry shop first."

"I didn't think it was one of the locals. I thought I was being crass, assuming it was someone from the outside."

"Outside?" I thought about it. "Oh. You mean outside of Palm Beach." I unleashed Sweet Pea, ran to get Aunt Mary's water and returned a few moments later.

I handed her a glass. *"I'm* not a Palm Beach resident."

She sipped the water and massaged Sweet Pea's neck. "Oh, yes you are. Now."

Worry crossed my mind, as it had done numerous times since Aunt Mary had given me the money for Canine Confections. "I hope now that Martha will be put behind bars but only for a moment my business takes an upswing."

She cupped my chin. "I have not one doubt."

After a minute, I helped Aunt Mary up so we could leave. "You drove yourself here?"

"That's right. I let Alice go. I caught her stealing a ring from my jewelry box."

I looked at her in disbelief. "She told me it was because you couldn't afford her anymore!"

My aunt let out a short laugh, then resumed careful steps to the front door. "I guess it's as good an excuse as any while she's explaining why she lost her job. She should know I have connections all over town."

I blinked up at her and at that word: *Connections.* Martha's lack of them was one reason—in her mind, anyway—she would be spending the foreseeable future in jail. I felt better that Aunt Mary's finances weren't so far gone that she had to get rid of her assistant, but I had to admit, I felt a little bad about Martha. Until I thought about Whitney's dead body on my floor.

"You know I'm not letting you drive back home tonight, right?" I asked.

"And you know I'm not your child ... *right?*" she answered.

We went back and forth and I finally won, mostly I think because it was getting late and she just wanted to shut me up.

"I'll figure something out to come back for your car in the morning," I said and loaded her and Sweet Pea into my car.

We drove home with the windows open. I hadn't even noticed my stomach had been clenched until we drove along Ocean Boulevard, I breathed in the salt air, and felt it release.

Once I settled Aunt Mary into the Big House and me and Sweet Pea into our cottage, I poured a mug of hot cocoa with both big *and* mini-marshmallows and snuggled in bed with Sweet Pea. I brought the mug to my mouth and paused when my cell vibrated a text notification.

Rick: Ready for that drink at HMF one night this week?

Me: Maybe.

I needed a minute. First, I needed to digest everything that happened and get Canine Confections firmly established as a fabulous dog bakery in the marvelous Palm Beach.

Rick: Can I call you now for a chat?

Me: When exactly did people start texting before calling?

Rick: Does that mean yes?

I set my cup of cocoa on my nightstand, nestled further into the down pillows of my bed, massaged Sweet Pea's velvet ears, and smiled as I thought about my answer.

THE END

Blue Blue Berry Berry Bun Buns

This recipe is from Chef Sarah Deters at the test kitchen of Three Dog Bakery, the original bakery for dogs.

Makes a dozen berry, berry delicious muffins

1 cup skim milk

¼ cup vegetable oil

1/3 cup honey

1 egg

2 1/3 cups white flour

4 tsp baking powder

1 tsp vanilla

1 ½ cups fresh blueberries

Preheat oven to 375 degrees.

- In mixing bowl, combine milk, oil and honey. Add egg and blend well.
- Combine flour and baking powder in a separate bowl and add to wet ingredients. Stir together thoroughly.
- Add vanilla and fold in blueberries.
- Grease a muffin tin and fill two thirds full.
- Bake for 20 – 25 minutes, or until a toothpick inserted in the center of a muffin comes out clean. Cool before serving and store in a sealed container.

Read the first chapter of

Book 2 in the Canine Confections Mystery Series

PAWS FOR ALARM

"My head feels wonky," Jenny said from her side of Patisserie of Palm Beach's patio table.

"Another headache?" I asked.

The manager of the pastry shop two doors down from Canine Confections seemed to be complaining a lot about headaches lately. I was beginning to worry.

She dismissed my question, swiveled her head up and down ritzy Worth Avenue and blinked at the morning light. "So, Samantha Armstrong," she said. "Here you are, here I am, and here is Sweet Pea …" She leaned down and scruffed my dog's fuzzy ears. "Where's everybody else?"

"No idea."

For the past month, a few of our fellow shopkeepers had been meeting for a good old-fashioned coffee klatch on the patio of the pastry shop. By this time of the morning, we were normally knocking back cappuccinos and discussing our latest marketing ideas or dating disasters.

Sweet Pea tilted her head so Jenny could reach the exact right spot behind her folded Labrador mix ears and licked her hand.

"She sure is affectionate," Jenny said.

"As long as you don't murder anybody."

Jenny's jaw dropped.

"That was blunt," I said and chuckled awkwardly. "I only meant the one person she never licked was the woman who killed Whitney." Whitney, the former owner of Patisserie—and of Sweet Pea—whom I had found dead on Canine Confections' floor a month ago. I had read that a flippant attitude was a way for the mind to digest awful things until it's ready to deal, but geez, my coldness sounded crass.

Jenny eyed me with suspicion but tucked a loose, sun-bleached strand of hair behind her ear and immediately turned her attention to the four empty chairs at the patio table. "So much for coffee klatch today."

"No!" I said with more feeling than the situation warranted.

Jenny raised her eyebrows.

Our coffee klatch had become a cozy gathering, something to count on. After all I had been through—moving to a new town where I felt as out of place as a dinosaur in a china shop, opening a dog bakery with what turned out to be my Aunt Mary's life savings, finding a dead body on the morning of my grand opening, and trying to drum up consistent business for the dog bakery everyone in Palm Beach thought of as a murder site—I wasn't ready to let go of my morning ritual with my new circle of friends.

"They'll show," I said firmly.

As if on cue, Dominique, the Palm Beach socialite who doesn't *work* on Worth Avenue but jogs on it like clockwork every morning, exited Patisserie's front door and plopped a pumpkin on the table.

"Happy Halloween to you, too," I said with a laugh and sipped my cappuccino.

Sweet Pea jumped up, kissed Dominique's calf one time, then returned to her spot next to me.

Jenny asked, "Doesn't taking the shortcut through the back door of Patisserie sort of defeat the purpose of getting your morning exercise?"

"I was on my way to my car parked back there when I saw Frederika's pumpkin display in front of her flower shop." Dominique shrugged one toned shoulder. "I couldn't resist buying one, but I didn't feel like lugging it around the building."

"You were going to miss coffee klatch?" Jenny asked.

Dominique nodded and winced as she pressed in on her 200-sit-ups-a-day abdomen with a hand that, by the look of the blisters, held a tennis racket a little too overzealously.

I laughed at the oversized gourd as large as a beach ball. "Is it big enough?"

"I thought one of you might want to use it for your bakeries. Make some pumpkin pie or something."

Jenny said, "Samantha owns a dog bakery. This is a pastry shop and it's for humans."

"Excuse me, Miss Semantics," Dominique replied.

Jenny said excitedly, "I think we should make a jack-o-lantern with it." She looked at me to get my take on the idea, then held a hand to her forehead and grimaced.

"Do whatever you want, I bought it to cheer myself up." Dominique pressed her hands into her stomach. "My stomach has been killing me. I must have eaten some bad sushi or something last night." She touched her fingers to her clavicle. "Plus, I lost my necklace during my jog."

"The one your grandmother gave you?" Jenny asked.

"The clasp was loose. I checked to make sure it was on while I jogged past Jimmy Choo, and when I felt for it in front of Starbucks, it was gone."

I licked the foamy cinnamon on my lips and started to jump up from my chair. "So let's go check the sidewalk between Jimmy Choo and Starbucks."

Dominique shook her head and drank from her water bottle. "I went back to check as soon as it started to get light out. It's not there."

I sat back down. "It would be funny if whoever picked it up is the same person who is stealing from the shops around here."

"Hilarious," Jenny responded.

Dominique twisted the cap of her water bottle back and forth like it was the thief's neck instead of an innocent plastic thingamabob. "One of these days, I'm going to find out who it is and have a little chat with them." The muscles in her biceps shifted with each twist of the cap.

"You keep saying that," Jenny said with a small smile.

"And I mean it."

Jenny and I exchanged nervous glances.

Dominique tilted the remains of her water bottle into her mouth with blistered fingers. "There's one person I see window-shopping every morning but I can't make out who it is. Medium-height, and they wear a coat, hat, and gloves, so I don't know who it is or what they're doing. They can't be jogging or walking with that get-up on. I called out to them yesterday and yelled that I'd find out who they were."

I set my cappuccino down on the saucer. "They're trying to be incognito? You think it's the thief?"

Dominique pressed her hands to her stomach again and sat down. "Who else?"

"You should tell the police," I said.

"Tell them what? 'Hey Officer, I see someone walking around in a coat at four a.m., and it might be the same person who is stealing from the shops.' I can see how that would go over."

"You can tell them you see someone strange walking around in a coat," I offered.

"They probably have better things to do than worry about another eccentric person in Palm Beach." Dominique slowly stood up while Jenny and I eyed her with concern. "The next time I see that weirdo in a coat lurking about, I'll knock them out before they know what hit them."

Dominique left us with the pumpkin as she re-entered Patisserie from the front to leave out the back.

Jenny picked up the monstrous orange gourd. "You okay if I take this and make a jack-o-lantern?"

"Sure, but won't it be rotten by the time Halloween comes next week?"

"Don't they sell something to prevent pumpkins from rotting so fast?"

"Don't ask me. The only thing I know about arts and crafts is that I can make an outline of a turkey by tracing my hand."

Jenny heaved the pumpkin up in her arms and headed to the front door of the pastry shop. "I guess everyone else is a no-show."

Sweet Pea instantly jumped to her feet when I stood up.

"Guess so. See you later, alligator," I said to Jenny and left with Sweet Pea.

My dog and I strolled two shops down to Canine Confections. "Why did Tracy miss coffee klatch?"

She stared up at me and lolled her tongue.

I tried to insert my key into the front door of Confections but the door opened an inch. It was not only *not* locked, but not even shut.

"We haven't been here yet this morning," I said to Sweet Pea. "I know I asked Tracy to lock up last night on our way out. Think she forgot?"

Sweet Pea tentatively wagged her tail at my questioning tone.

I froze when a hand pressed on my left shoulder from behind, then whirled around breathlessly, feeling like a ghost had floated over my grave.

"Geez!" I shouted at Tracy, giggling in front of me. "What are you, twelve years old?" I smiled in spite of myself.

"Nope," she answered. "Twenty-seven, like you."

"You'd never know it," I grumbled. "Surprises like that are what I *don't* need during the spookiest time of the year."

Sweet Pea waved her tail from side to side and licked Tracy's hands in greeting.

I swung Confections' door wide …

… and my jaw dropped at the second surprise of the day.

CPSIA information can be obtained
at www.ICGtesting.com
Printed in the USA
LVHW091153170421
684783LV00022B/227

9 781944 066376